CUBBY

Jyl Glenn

Paperback ISBN: 979-8-9919908-2-0

Cover Art by Ruth Anna Evans

Edited by Darren C. Perdue

Formatting by Jyl Glenn

CONTENTS

Prologue   1

Chapter 1   3

Chapter 2   16

Chapter 3   28

Chapter 4   39

Chapter 5   50

Chapter 6   64

Chapter 7   75

Chapter 8   84

Chapter 9   99

Chapter 10   113

Chapter 11   126

Chapter 12   140

Chapter 13   151

Acknowledgments   157

About the Author   159

Also by Jyl Glenn   161

PROLOGUE

I don't sleep anymore.

Not that I ever really did. I wait—quiet as dust. They always think the silence means I'm gone. That's their first mistake.

It's strange what people leave behind. A hair in the carpet. A fingerprint on the glass. A sound in the walls that doesn't stop just because no one's listening. Pain. Trauma.

You'd be amazed at what a house can hold if no one tells it not to.

They always come with their boxes and their paint and their bright little plans. They talk like they've won something. Like they belong. I let them think that.

At first.

They clean the windows. Hang pictures. Pick colors for the walls. The dog barks at nothing and

1

they laugh. They sleep through the first creak of the floorboards, the first shadow in the wrong corner. They say the air's dry. They say old houses groan. They say everything is fine.

But the joy never lasts here. Not really.

It fades at the edges.

It seeps out through the cracks.

That's when they start to notice. The cold spot at the top of the stairs. The objects that don't stay put. The chair that rocks once and stops. An animal or child staring at something they can't see, going still in a way that makes them stop breathing, too.

They blame each other. Then the house. Then the history. But they never get it right.

They never ask what's *waiting*.

Some things get left behind for a reason.

But I don't mind. I've always been patient.

Every child needs a friend. Someone who never leaves.

Someone who listens.

Why shouldn't it be me?

CHAPTER
ONE

The house sat on a gentle rise about fifteen minutes outside the city. It was close enough for errands and late-night takeout, but far enough to feel like the start of something new. Emma liked this place. It struck a balance she hadn't realized she was craving, the kind of place where you could raise a baby without sirens at night. The road curved through wind-worn trees before opening up into a small gravel driveway flanked by dry grass and a mailbox that leaned a little to the left.

Daisy barked once from the back seat as Caleb put the car in park. "We made it," he said, half-smiling at Emma as he turned off the engine.

Emma let out a long breath, relieved they were finally moving in. Her hands rested on her pregnant belly like she was steadying something inside her that had nothing to do with the baby.

The house was older than it looked—tall, thin windows, faded blue paint, and a porch that needed sanding—but it had charm. Not the HGTV kind; that was all lighting tricks and staged fruit bowls. This house had the kind that made you want to stay awhile. It looked and felt like it had memories. Emma wasn't a fan of the half-scorched barn, but Caleb had insisted he could fix it.

They'd been looking for months, narrowing down choices between sprawling suburbs and over-priced condos, until this listing appeared late one night. There were minimal photographs on the listing. A place that seemed to want to be left alone. Which, somehow, made Emma want it more. They had called their realtor right away, toured the house the next day, and made an offer that night.

They started unloading right away. Emma moved slowly, her center of gravity thrown off by her expanding belly. Caleb kept glancing at her, trying not to look like he was hovering.

Inside, the hardwood floors were scuffed but solid. The living room opened into a small kitchen that smelled faintly of cedar and something older— maybe mothballs, or the stale tang of long-unused heating vents. The walls had once been painted a warm cream, but years of grime had turned them a kind of yellow gray. Still, there was potential. Light pooled in through the front windows, soft and gold. Emma could already envision what it would look like when they were finished with it.

The nursery-to-be was tucked down the hall, with a single window and peeling wallpaper in pale yellow stripes. Emma ran her hand along the windowsill. The whole room needed a good cleaning and repainting, but she didn't mind. The room was quiet in a way that suggested it had been waiting for sound again. *The mint green we picked out will be perfect.*

While Caleb wrestled with a box of bathroom supplies, Emma wandered. The upstairs had been converted to a giant primary bedroom with a full ensuite bath.

Someone put a lot of effort into this room, Emma thought as she looked around.

In the hall, there was a smaller door between the storage closets. It opened onto the attic stairs.

She hesitated at the bottom, looking up into the dim space. The air had a dry, still quality, like it had been sealed for years. She climbed slowly, one hand on the rail, and pushed open the door at the top.

The attic wasn't scary, not exactly. Just quiet. Dust floated in thin rays of light from a single pane window. Boxes were stacked against the far wall, along with a few old pieces of furniture draped in gray sheets. There was a door, but when Emma jiggled the knob, it wouldn't open. *I hope they gave us a key for that at closing*. And then, tucked in the back corner, under the sloped edge of the roof, something caught her eye—a cedar chest. It sat low to the ground; its brass hinges dulled with age but not rusted.

Emma knelt, brushing a fine layer of dust off the lid. It opened without resistance.

Inside, nestled against the smooth wood, was a teddy bear. Soft brown fur, glassy black eyes, and a perfectly tied blue velvet bow. No dust. No damage. It looked like it had just been placed there, carefully, intentionally, like it was meant to be a house-warming gift.

Emma blinked. Her first instinct wasn't fear. It was a glimmer of recognition, like the bear had been meant for them. She reached in and lifted it out. It was heavier than she expected. Warm, even. Not from the sun—there was no sunlight on the chest.

"Aren't you adorable!" she said to the bear and gave him a little boop on the nose.

"Emma? The moving truck is here." Caleb's voice echoed from downstairs.

"Coming!" she called, tucking the bear under her arm.

She paused once at the top of the stairs, looking back at the cedar chest. Empty now.

Downstairs, Caleb was directing the movers where to put boxes and furniture.

"Look what I found upstairs," Emma said.

He turned. "In the bedroom?"

"Nope. In the attic!" She held out the bear. "He's so clean. Looks brand new."

Caleb took it, inspected it, then handed it back. "Soft! Kind of creepy, though. But cute, I guess?"

"He's not creepy, Caleb. He's an adorable little teddy bear. His name is Cubby."

"You named him already?"

Emma smiled and shrugged. "He seems like a Cubby. Plus, it's written on the tag in marker." She turned the bear over to show him. "I'm going to put him in the nursery. He's perfect for the baby."

She went down the hall and into the nursery, pleased to see the movers had already brought in her rocking chair. She placed the bear in the chair before heading back to the car for another small box.

✖✖✖✖✖✖✖

A FEW DAYS LATER, Caleb was inside unpacking boxes, cursing gently every time he grabbed a box and found a silly label and no rhyme or reason to the box's contents.

"Dammit, Em," he shook his head. "The souls of my enemies? Supercali-FRAGILE-istic? Really?"

Emma was laughing so hard she had tears running down her cheeks. "Packing sucks! I had to find a way to make it a little bit fun. Also, that box *is* super fragile, thank you very much."

"At least one of us is having fun," he chuckled.

"Sorry, not sorry. I'm going to go out on the porch and get some fresh air. Wanna join me?"

"Sure, be out in a few."

The sun was just starting to set behind the hills when Emma stepped onto the porch with a mug of herbal tea in hand. The air was warm and lazy, buzzing with cicadas and thick with the scent of cut grass. Emma leaned on the porch railing, letting her gaze drift across the property—over the broken fence line, the shed, and the burned-out barn that seemed darker than it should have in the golden hour light. *We really need to tear that thing down.*

Then she saw her.

A woman, maybe in her late sixties, was walking up the gravel driveway, moving with the purpose of someone who'd walked this road before. She wore jeans, a faded flannel, and carried nothing but a plastic grocery bag that crinkled with each step.

Emma stepped forward. "Hi there. Can I help you?"

The woman didn't answer right away. She stopped a few feet from the steps, eyes scanning the house, then Emma.

"You're the new owners?"

Emma nodded. "Yes, hello, I'm Emma. We just moved in a couple of days ago."

The woman's face didn't change, but something in her jaw tightened. "My name's Margaret. I live down the road. I grew up here."

She reached into the grocery bag and pulled out something wrapped in foil. "I brought banana bread. My mama always said it's bad luck not to welcome new folks. And I wanted to give you my number. But—" She hesitated, then handed the bread over. "This place . . . it's got a long memory."

Emma took the parcel and the slip of paper with the phone number, feeling the warmth still clinging to the bottom. "That's really kind of you."

Margaret nodded, but her eyes drifted past Emma, toward the top of the house.

"I'm telling you to be careful with what you find up there. This house holds onto things."

Before Emma could respond, Margaret turned and started walking back the way she came. Emma stood there, unsettled, watching her go. The banana bread felt heavier than it should have. When the woman was out of sight, she dropped the bread in the trash bin but tucked the number in her pocket to put in her phone, just in case. *Sorry, lady,* she thought. *I'm not eating anything from a stranger's kitchen.*

THAT NIGHT, they ate pizza on the floor of the living room, surrounded by unopened boxes and half-built furniture. Caleb made a joke about haunted toilets as he tossed a paper plate into an empty moving box.

Emma laughed, but her gaze drifted down the hallway toward the nursery.

Cubby sat in the rocking chair, perfectly still, his glass eyes reflecting just a sliver of hallway light.

She didn't mention the woman. Not yet.

Neither of them noticed Daisy staring from the kitchen—ears back, tail stiff, her eyes locked on the nursery door.

Emma leaned back against the wall, hand resting on her belly. The baby shifted gently, just a flutter. She closed her eyes and tried to listen to the silence, to settle into it. But the house didn't feel as quiet now. When she opened her eyes again, the hallway seemed darker than it had been a moment ago.

She stood, slowly, stretching out her back. "I'm going to head to bed," she said.

Caleb nodded, distracted, scrolling through his phone. "I'll be in soon."

Emma lingered in the doorway of the nursery for just a moment, one hand on the frame.

Cubby was still there. "You are so cute. Baby Otis is going to love you forever," she whispered.

She pulled the door almost closed, leaving it

open just a crack. Then she headed upstairs to bed. Behind her, the rocking chair gave a single, gentle creak. And then silence.

1961

RICHARD CARVER SAT cross-legged on the cold wooden floor, his knees pulled tight to his chest, arms wrapped around them like a brace. The room was quiet except for the wind pushing through a crack in the single-pane window. It whistled faintly, high-pitched, like a song trying to get in.

There was nothing on the walls. No posters, no pictures. Just peeling wallpaper. The corners of the ceiling had dark stains that looked like bruises. A single naked bulb dangled from the ceiling.

He'd been sitting there for hours, but he didn't mind.

He'd gotten good at waiting.

The floor beneath him was cold, but he didn't shift. If he kept perfectly still, he forgot how uncomfortable it was.

He didn't look up when his mother entered his attic room. He'd heard her come home from wherever she had been. He'd heard her clattering around in the kitchen, making instant coffee. *Gross.* He knew she would either come yell at him for something or forget he existed. He had hoped for the latter and his heart sank a little bit when he heard her coming up the stairs.

The door creaked open, then groaned halfway shut behind her. She never stayed very long. Too much time in the room and she'd start to fidget.

She had a cigarette clamped between her lips, one hand on her hip, the other holding a plain brown grocery bag—half-crumpled, like it had been kicked around before she got it home.

No card. No wrapping paper. No cupcakes. No smile. No happy birthday.

She walked to the small table in the center of the room, the old wobbly one with the faded yellow top and burn marks along the edge and swept his toys to the floor. Richard could see something was peeking out of a torn corner of the bag. Something plush and brown. Soft-looking. She tossed it and it landed on the table with a muffled *thump*.

"That's all you get," she muttered, stubbing the cigarette out on his table. "And don't go telling folks I never got you anything."

She didn't wait for him to respond. She was already turning away, flicking the lighter for another smoke.

By the time she stepped back into the hall, the

only sign she'd ever been there was a smear of ash on the table and a fading trace of drugstore perfume.

Richard waited.

He counted to twenty in his head and then again for good measure.

Sometimes she would come back because she remembered something to be mad about, or because she changed her mind. Once she had yanked a toy out of his hands and threw it in the garbage. "You don't play with it right," she'd said. So, he waited.

When he reached twenty the second time, he stood up slowly and approached the table like he was afraid it would disappear.

He tore open the paper bag to find a stuffed bear. He picked it up with reverence. One glass eye glinted in the dim light of the room. Its fur was light brown, spotless, and as soft as a cloud. The bow was velvet and a perfect shade of blue.

Richard turned it over and over, examining it, like he was trying to commit it to memory before it disappeared. It was a nice bear. Not cheap. Not worn. *New.* His mother never gave him anything new or nice. He stared at its stitched nose, its neat little paws, the slight curve of the mouth that looked, in the right light, almost like a smile. And it felt warm despite the fall chill.

"You're mine now," he whispered.

He held the bear gently to his chest, the way someone might cradle a new puppy. It fit there perfectly, the bear's head tucked beneath his chin, as if it had always been meant for this.

"I'll take care of you," he said softly. "I promise."

There was no reply, but Richard didn't expect one.

From the hallway, he heard the sharp rattle of a spoon in a mug and the clatter of the faucet running too long. His mother, probably making her instant coffee again, forgetting she already had. She would sit at the table in her slip, drinking half, letting the rest go cold.

He walked back to his place on the floor and sat again, the bear still in his arms. Then he began to rock. Slowly, side to side, the way he did when the shouting downstairs used to scare him, when his father's boots stomped heavy like they were going to break through the floorboards. That part was over. His father was long gone.

The fear still lingered, but it wasn't loud anymore. Just low. Constant. A hum in the bones. The tears came quietly. He didn't sob. He didn't shake. His face pressed into the bear's light brown fur, soaking it. He didn't care. The bear felt soft. Not just soft. *Safe.* The kind of safe he couldn't remember ever having before.

His mother never came back to check on him. She never asked if he liked it, never watched him open it, never told him happy birthday. Maybe she forgot. Or maybe she didn't care. Downstairs, he heard the TV click on. Some game show his mother wouldn't pay attention to, but was still, somehow, more important than him. But it didn't matter. He had a friend now. He didn't sleep, not yet. His new friend needed a name. He sat, rocking, the bear held tight, his cheek against its head.

"I won't let anyone hurt you, little bear cub," he said, voice barely above a breath. He held the bear out at arm's length and looked into its eyes. "That's it! Cubby. Your name is Cubby! Do you like it?"

"You don't have to answer," Richard whispered as he grabbed a marker and wrote CUBBY on the tag. "I saw you blink."

TWO

The first few days in the new house were calm.

Emma unpacked slowly, taking breaks often, her feet swelling more quickly than they used to. Caleb tackled the heavier tasks—reassembling furniture, fixing a leaky faucet in the kitchen, changing out lightbulbs in fixtures that buzzed or flickered. Even Daisy seemed to be adjusting, though she still gave the nursery a wide berth. She would pause at the doorway, whine quietly, and walk away.

It didn't go unnoticed.

"She's probably just thrown off by all the change," Caleb offered, scratching behind Daisy's ears. "New smells. New sounds. She'll be fine."

Emma nodded, but she kept a careful eye on the dog all the same. Daisy never barked. Never growled. But she avoided the nursery, as though something in that room made her skin crawl.

Emma caught herself watching the nursery, too. Sometimes she passed the door and felt a tiny jolt of apprehension, like she'd forgotten something or was about to. But the room was always still. Quiet. The kind of quiet that should feel safe but didn't.

Emma didn't notice it at first. She walked past the nursery on her way to the laundry room, hands full of towels, when she paused and frowned. The rocking chair sat empty.

She leaned inside, checked the crib, the corner shelf, and the floor.

No Cubby.

Her stomach tightened, an irrational twist of unease she tried to brush off. She found the bear in the upstairs hallway, sitting upright against the wall like someone had gently placed him there.

"Caleb?" she called, walking to the bedroom. "Did you move the bear?"

He looked up from his laptop. "What bear?"

"Cubby. The one I found in the attic."

He furrowed his brow. "No. Why would I do that?"

Emma held the bear up. "He wasn't in the nursery. He was sitting outside the door."

Caleb shrugged. "Maybe Daisy dragged him out?"

But when Emma looked down, Daisy was sitting

at the bottom of the stairs, head low, ears flat, staring up at them with a wide, still expression. She didn't blink. Didn't wag her tail. Just stared.

Emma carried Cubby back to the nursery and set him on the chair. She didn't say anything else.

Three days passed. The weather warmed slightly, and Emma spent more time on the porch, drinking iced tea and watching the trees. She tried to read, but her thoughts wandered back to the attic. Back to Margaret. Back to that line about the house holding onto things.

She hadn't told Caleb about the conversation. It had seemed like a strange courtesy visit, neighborly and eccentric. But Margaret's words stuck with her in the quiet moments, when the house creaked in places she wasn't in, or when the nursery door she swore she had closed stood cracked open again.

On Thursday morning, she walked into the kitchen to find Cubby sitting on one of the chairs at the table. Propped up perfectly. Facing the window.

She stood frozen for a moment, tea kettle in hand.

"Caleb!"

He came in a minute later, rubbing sleep from his eyes. "What's up?"

She pointed.

He stared at the bear. "Okay, that's weird. Damn dog."

"You didn't move him?"

"No."

"Well, Daisy can't open doors."

They both turned toward the dog, who was lying in the entryway with her nose tucked under her paw.

"You're sure you didn't maybe forget moving him?" Caleb asked, not unkindly—but with that edge, the one he got when he thought she was being hormonal.

Emma shook her head. "I remember putting him back in the chair. I haven't touched him since."

Caleb picked Cubby up, inspected him, then placed him back in the nursery. He shut the door firmly behind him.

Later that day, Emma passed by the room and opened the door to check.

Cubby was still there. Right where he'd been placed.

But that night, after dinner, when she walked by again to put a basket of laundry away—he was gone.

She found him this time on the floor of the bathroom, sitting between the toilet and the wall.

"Caleb."

He appeared instantly. "Again?"

Emma just pointed.

He sighed, rubbing his face. "Look, babe, I know you're tired. And the move's been a lot. But it's just a stuffed animal."

"I didn't move him!"

"Okay. Maybe it fell and Daisy nosed it around."

"She won't even go in the room."

"It has to be the dog, Em. Because if it's not the dog, then what is it?"

Emma didn't answer. She picked up Cubby and returned him to the nursery in silence.

That night, they left the nursery door slightly ajar. And in the morning, Cubby was on the windowsill. Emma didn't bother asking Caleb about it.

✖✖✖✖✖✖

EMMA STARTED DREAMING MORE OFTEN. Vague things—shadows behind doors, the sensation of being watched, a soft pressure on her chest like something small and heavy was resting there. She never remembered the endings.

Sometimes she woke with the feeling that the nursery door had opened during the night, that someone had walked the hallway barefoot, slow and quiet.

Other times, she questioned herself. Had she left the door open? Had she moved the bear and forgotten? Pregnancy brain was real. Maybe her mind was exaggerating little things into big ones.

Still, Daisy refused to go near the room.

Over the weekend, Caleb fixed the garage door and hung new shelves in the laundry room. Emma organized the kitchen drawers and caught up on emails. They didn't talk about the bear. Not directly.

But the house felt different. Heavier. Like it was paying attention.

Daisy barked once—just once—late Sunday night, a sharp, sudden sound that jolted Emma awake. But when she and Caleb checked around the house, everything was still.

Except for the gentle sway of the rocking chair in the nursery.

Emma touched the bear's ear and found it warm.

XXXXXXX

THE NEXT MORNING, Emma folded the laundry in silence while Caleb made coffee without a word. The house felt still, but not empty—like someone else was waiting for them to say it out loud. Neither of them did. Daisy sat in the kitchen doorway, watching the hallway with quiet tension. Every so often, her ears flicked toward the nursery. Emma avoided the room most of the day.

When she finally passed by on her way upstairs, the door was open again. She was sure she'd left it closed. Cubby sat in the chair. Exactly where she'd left him. Exactly where he should be. She pulled the door closed without going in.

She grabbed a book and sat down to read, but she kept thinking about the bear. About the warmth. About the quiet, creeping certainty that something was out of place, and had been since the moment they stepped into the house.

The words on the page blurred. She re-read the same paragraph five times before giving up. The silence around her felt stretched too thin, like plastic wrap pulled too tight. She glanced toward the hall-way, toward the closed nursery door.

A creak came from the pipes above her. Or the ceiling. Or the stairs. She couldn't tell. She listened hard, breath shallow, and told herself it was noth-ing. All houses made sounds. Old ones never knew when to stay quiet. But this house didn't creak the way others did. It waited. And every so often, it sighed.

She thought about telling Caleb again. Really telling him—about Margaret, about the feeling that Cubby wasn't just a weird leftover toy. But he already thought she was spiraling. Hormonal. Overly imaginative. She didn't want to feed that look he gave her sometimes, the quiet doubt just behind his eyes.

So, she stayed quiet.

And down the hall, behind the nursery door, the rocking chair began to move.

✕✕✕✕✕✕

1963

RICHARD STOOD at the edge of the playground hill, his sneakers buried in dry, brittle grass that crunched beneath his soles. He clutched Cubby tightly to his chest, the small stuffed bear nestled under his chin, its eyes reflecting the dull overcast sky.

Behind him, the playground was alive with chaos. Kids shouted, chasing one another through and around the monkey bars and swing sets. Girls jumped rope in a tight rhythm near the hopscotch squares, and somewhere near the slide, a whistle blew. But Richard didn't move. He stood apart from the noise, face still, gaze fixed on the wavering tree-tops that lined the field beyond the fence. He liked it better up here. It was quieter. Safer. Most days, the other kids left him and Cubby alone.

Cubby rested perfectly still in his arms. No one else was allowed to touch him. Not even his mother. Cubby wasn't a toy. He was a friend.

Richard murmured to him, voice barely louder than the wind. "They won't bother us today. It's our birthday!" But he was wrong.

Billy Donaldson was already halfway up the hill, swaggering in his too-big boots, lips twisted into a crooked smile. He was the kind of boy who got bored easily and always looked for someone smaller to ruin.

"There he is," Billy called out, loud enough for the kids below to hear. "Baby Richie and his little baby bear."

Richard said nothing. He didn't move. He shifted his grip on Cubby.

Billy kept climbing, dragging his boots through the dirt and grass, loud on purpose. "What's the matter? You hiding up here with your teddy? You gonna cry if I take it away?"

He was close now—too close.

Richard could smell the sour milk on Billy's breath, see the chapped skin on his knuckles. He'd done this before. Not here, not like this, but enough to know how it would go.

Billy reached out.

"Don't touch him," Richard said.

Billy grinned. "I just wanna hold it."

"No."

"Don't be such a freak."

Then he grabbed Cubby by the leg and pulled.

Richard didn't loosen his grip, not even a little, but Billy's tug was strong. The bear jerked downward, and Richard went down with him. There was a small pop. Not from the bear, but from somewhere deeper, something between his ears and his chest. A wrongness.

The other kids came to see what was happening. They all laughed. Billy taunted, "Baby Richie and his stupid baby bear! They smell like ketchup and dirty underwear!"

Richard picked up a rock and his arm came up like it was someone else's. A clean arc. The rock struck Billy's face, catching his nose dead-center.

There was a crunch. Sharp and wet.

Billy went down fast, knees folding beneath him as he screamed.

His hands flew to his face, and he rolled on the hill, kicking wildly in the dirt, shrieking in short, broken gasps.

Richard stood perfectly still.

Cubby was safe. Still in his arms. Still untouched.

The children began to scream.

Teachers screamed at them to stop and came running.

Richard didn't flinch. His breathing slowed. He watched Billy flail and bleed, and he didn't feel regret or fear.

He felt *right*.

A shadow fell across him. One of the adults, Ms. Fowler, his mean second-grade teacher, rushed up the hill, skirt billowing around her knees.

"Richard? What happened here?!"

Billy wailed louder. "He hit me! He hit me in the nose! He-he went crazy!"

Richard looked up at her. His voice didn't waver.

"He tried to hurt my friend."

She blinked. "Your friend?"

Richard nodded, slowly.

She followed his gaze, not to the bleeding boy at her feet or any of the other children, but to the bear in his arms.

Her expression shifted. First confusion, then something else. Something condescending.

"I see," she said, though it was clear she didn't.

She told him to wait by the principal's office while they called his mother.

✗✗✗✗✗✗✗

THAT NIGHT, Richard sat alone in the attic room above the garage, knees pulled to his chest, Cubby cradled beneath his chin. No light was on. He liked the dark. It made things feel even.

Below him, he could hear the echo of his mother's voice through the floorboards, tinny and sharp as she argued on the phone with someone.

Richard tuned it out.

The attic walls were close and quiet. Dust motes drifted in a shaft of moonlight from the single window above the boxes.

He held Cubby gently. Pressed his cheek to the soft plush.

"I told you," Richard whispered. "I'll protect you. I promise we'll have a better birthday next year."

He rocked slightly, back and forth, the old boards creaking in rhythm. Outside, the wind moved through the trees like a voice trying to reach him. But he already had someone to talk to.

He didn't need anyone else.

CHAPTER
THREE

For a few weeks, everything was quiet.

Cubby stayed in the nursery. Daisy still avoided the room, but Emma stopped noticing it as much. The baby kicked more. Caleb smiled easier. They settled into something that almost resembled routine.

Emma still checked the bear every morning— but more out of habit than dread. He never moved. Never even tilted.

Eventually, she stopped checking.

They painted the nursery mint green, just like Emma had imagined. Caleb installed floating shelves and a blackout curtain. Emma spent afternoons folding tiny onesies and lining them up in drawers, even though the baby wouldn't need most of them for months. She liked the rhythm of it, the careful repetition. It made her feel in control.

She made a list every morning—laundry, dishes, phone calls—and crossed things off like she was keeping the house in check, as if the structure alone could protect them. She spent more time in the kitchen, baking muffins she didn't even want to eat, just to make the place smell warm.

Caleb worked from the dining room, laptop surrounded by coffee mugs and stacks of paperwork. They discussed the best way to hang the baby mobile. He teased her for organizing the spice rack alphabetically. She teased him back for pretending he didn't know where things were, hence, why she alphabetized things.

At night, she slept deeper than she had in months.

That was when the dreams started again.

❌❌❌❌❌❌

THEY WEREN'T NIGHTMARES. Not exactly. But they were strange and left her feeling unsettled.

A little boy, maybe seven or eight, sat cross-legged on a wooden floor she didn't recognize, holding Cubby in his lap. His back was always turned. His clothes were plain—too plain, like something from another time. His hair stuck out in soft tufts behind his ears. He rocked slightly, whis-

29

pering to the bear in a voice too low for Emma to hear.

She wanted to speak to him. Wanted to ask where he came from, why he looked so sad. But the dream never gave her control. She was just there, watching.

Sometimes, the boy glanced over his shoulder—not enough for her to see his face, but just enough for her to feel seen. And each time, just as she began to reach toward him, she would wake up.

Other nights, she dreamt of Cubby alone in the crib, the room dim, the shadows moving strangely. Sometimes his eyes blinked. Not the natural kind of blink, but deliberate—slow, precise, as if watching her sleep.

She didn't tell Caleb about the dreams. She didn't want him to give her *that* look. They were just dreams, after all.

🐻🐻🐻🐻🐻🐻

ONE RAINY AFTERNOON, while Caleb was under the kitchen sink trying to fix a slow but annoying leak, Emma walked past the nursery and froze.

Cubby was in the crib.

Not slumped or tossed, but placed—his head resting on a pillow, arms at his sides, the blue velvet bow perfectly centered. The air in the room felt different. Still, but heavy. Like stepping into a memory that didn't belong to her. She stared at the bear for a long time before calling Caleb in. He came up behind her and followed her gaze.

"I'll put him back in the attic," he said quietly.

She nodded.

He didn't ask how Cubby got there. She didn't offer a theory. The silence between them was thick, and oddly mutual. As if neither of them wanted to hear the other confirm what they were both starting to feel.

Caleb carried the bear upstairs while Emma waited at the bottom, arms crossed. She heard the creak of the attic door, the soft sound of the chest opening and closing, then Caleb's footsteps returning. They didn't talk any more about it.

That night, Emma stayed up reading until her eyes burned. Caleb fell asleep with the remote in his hand, the TV still glowing blue in the corner. Neither of them said goodnight.

🧸🧸🧸🧸🧸🧸🧸

A WEEK PASSED.

Then two.

The bear didn't return.

Emma told herself it was over. That it had all been stress and hormones and an overactive imagination. *Maybe it was the dog.* She started sleeping through the night again. The dreams faded. The nursery, freshly painted and sunlit, felt like a real space now—bright, expectant, almost normal.

They went to the farmers market one Saturday. Went out to dinner with some friends. Caleb picked out a tiny onesie that said *New to the Crew* and Emma almost cried when he held it up in the aisle of Target. Everything felt lighter again. Safer.

Still, the memory of Cubby in the crib lingered, soft as dust on a windowsill.

On a quiet Wednesday morning, after Caleb left for a hardware run, Emma climbed the stairs to the attic alone. She hadn't gone up since they moved in. She told herself she just needed to make sure the bear was still there.

She stood still for several minutes, breathing softly, as if any motion might stir something awake. The attic was exactly as they'd left it. Boxes. Old furniture. The unsettling locked door leading to who knows what. The chest. The dust hadn't moved. No footprints. No disturbance. She took a deep breath and lifted the lid. There was Cubby, just as he should be. *You're really losing it, girl.*

She made her way back down the stairs and pulled the door closed behind her. She didn't tell Caleb she'd gone up there. That night, she had another odd dream.

This time the boy was facing her. Still distant,

still blurry. But there was something new—his hands trembled slightly as he clutched Cubby. His mouth moved quickly, as though whispering secrets too fast to catch.

He looked scared. Emma reached for him, and this time, he flinched. She woke with a jolt, her hand outstretched into the empty dark. The room was still. No movement, no sound. Caleb lay beside her, undisturbed, one arm draped over his eyes.

Emma sat up slowly, her heart thudding hard against her ribs. She looked at her hand, still half-raised, as if she'd expected something to be there. Someone. She lowered it to her lap and waited—for what, she didn't know. Nothing came. Eventually, she lay back down but kept her eyes open.

She didn't quite trust the dark to stay where it belonged.

🧸🧸🧸🧸🧸🧸

TWO NIGHTS LATER, just after midnight, Emma woke to a faint, warped sound drifting through the house.

A lullaby.

Familiar, but wrong. Like it was playing through a music box that had been left out in the rain. The tune stuttered and dragged, slowed in unnatural places. It sounded almost sleepy. Almost human. She sat up in bed, heart pounding.

"Caleb," she whispered. "Do you hear that?"

He stirred, groggy. "What?"

"Shhh. Listen."

They sat in the dark together, straining. But the house was silent.

After a moment, Caleb sighed and rolled over. "It's nothing, babe. Probably wind through the vent."

Emma didn't answer. She slid out of bed and tiptoed down the hall. The nursery door was shut. She hadn't closed it. Her hand hesitated on the knob. The cool brass felt like it had been waiting for her. She opened it slowly. Everything was in place.

Crib. Shelves. Rocking chair. No music. No movement. Cubby wasn't there. She checked the floor. The closet. The hallway.

Nothing.

Still, she couldn't shake the feeling that she had interrupted something.

She stood in the nursery doorway for a long time, staring into the shadows, listening for the next note. But the song was over. Still, she didn't move.

The crib stood quiet. The mobile above it—little felt clouds and stars—swayed gently, though the window was shut and the air was still. Emma watched it turn. One slow rotation. Then another. She couldn't tell if it had already been moving when she walked in or if opening the door had disturbed it.

She crossed the room and reached out a hand, steadying the mobile. It stilled under her fingers. The silence that followed felt heavier than before.

On the dresser, her to-do list sat in perfect order. Finish baby registry. Send baby shower invites. Buy more prenatal vitamins. Every task was normal, necessary, a tiny piece of the life she and Caleb were building. But at that moment, it felt like pretending. Like decorating a stage that had already been marked for something else.

She looked around the room—the fresh paint, the carefully arranged baby books, stacks of diapers and wipes, the folded blankets. It was all supposed to mean *safe*. But she didn't feel safe.

She didn't feel watched, exactly. Not in the way horror movies promised you would. No breath on the back of her neck. No shadow in the mirror. Just the echo of a presence that seemed to grow quieter the more she tried to find it.

She turned to leave, pausing with her hand on the doorknob. Then, just as she was pulling the door closed, she thought she heard something faint. The soft creak of fabric shifting. Like something settling into a seat.

Or lying down to rest.

She stood there for a moment, her hand on the doorknob, listening. The rustling had been so clear. Not loud, but definite. Real. She slowly opened the door again. The nursery was still. The mobile wasn't spinning. The shadows hadn't moved. Nothing in the crib. Nothing on the floor.

"No bear, thank goodness." she mumbled. "You need to get a grip," she told herself. Emma closed the door completely, careful not to let it latch too hard.

And for the rest of the night, she left the hallway light on.

✖✖✖✖✖✖

1965

RICHARD SAT on his bedroom floor, Cubby propped up beside him. He was ten now. The walls were still bare, wallpaper peeling in long strips like shed skin. The carpet had once been a soft blue but was now threadbare and matted down with dirt. The only light came from a naked bulb overhead, buzzing faintly like an irritated insect.

His knees were drawn up; arms wrapped around them. He stared blankly ahead, blinking slow and deliberate. Cubby leaned against his side, its stitched smile crooked and comforting.

Footsteps thundered up the stairs—heavy, angry, erratic. The door slammed open. His mother stood in the doorway, her face red, her makeup smeared, the cigarette between her fingers bent and soggy.

"Where's my ferret?!" she barked. "Three goddamn days it's been gone!"

She never asked him about his day at school. She didn't even wish him a happy birthday.

Richard put his arm around the bear and pulled Cubby close.

She stormed in, reeking of gin and hairspray. Her eyes darted around the room before locking onto him. "You did something to it, didn't you? Just like the neighbor's rabbit. Don't think I don't know."

Her voice cracked with fury. She marched over and grabbed his face, fingers like talons on his jaw. "Say it! Say what you did!"

Richard's eyes never left hers. They didn't blink.

"It was hurting him," he whispered.

Her brow furrowed. "What? Who?"

He didn't answer. His grip on Cubby tightened until his knuckles whitened.

She slapped him across the face, the sound echoing in the room. He didn't cry out. He barely flinched. She stormed out, muttering curses as she went.

Richard sat there, cheek reddened, breathing slow and even. Then he turned to Cubby and smiled faintly.

"She doesn't understand. You're the only one who loves me, so I had to get you *something*."

He peeled back a loose floorboard and pulled out a shoebox. It was covered in duct tape, but dark stains had bled through in places. He turned it slowly in his hands, then set it between him and Cubby.

"Happy birthday, Cubby."

He pressed his forehead to the bear's and whispered something too soft to hear.

The bulb overhead flickered once, then held steady.

FOUR

Emma dreamed she was sinking—something heavy pressing into her chest, pinning her down. She couldn't move. Couldn't breathe. Her arms felt locked to her sides.

She woke with a sharp gasp, heart racing.

She opened her eyes and looked around. The room was dark and still; the sheets twisted around her legs. Her arms ached like she had been lifting heavy things, something soft clutched to her chest.

She looked down. It was not her pillow.

Cubby was in her arms.

She was holding him like a child might hug a favorite stuffed toy. His glassy eyes stared up at her, and the blue velvet bow around his neck was slightly askew.

She froze. For one terrible second, she couldn't

move. She stared at the bear, heart pounding, brain lagging behind her senses.

She hadn't brought him into the room. She hadn't touched him since Caleb had put him in the attic. She didn't remember getting out of bed. Didn't remember retrieving him. And she knew Caleb wouldn't have brought him back.

And yet here he was. Pressed gently to her chest, as if he belonged there.

She rolled slowly out of bed, holding the bear at arm's length. She set him down on the night-stand. She didn't scream. Didn't wake Caleb. Just stared.

In the morning, Caleb stood in front of the open fridge, bare-chested and sleepy-eyed, pouring milk into his coffee.

Emma sat at the kitchen table, elbows on the wood, hands wrapped around her mug. "He was in our bed."

Caleb blinked, then blinked again. "What?"

"Cubby. I woke up with him in my arms."

Caleb slowly set the milk down. "Are you sure you didn't get up? Maybe you were half-asleep."

"I'm sure."

He crossed his arms, rubbing one hand over his mouth. "I didn't touch him. He should still be in the attic."

Emma just looked at him.

Caleb exhaled and turned toward the stairs.

"Okay. I'll take him back up. Before anyone gets here."

She nodded. "Thanks."

She didn't watch him go, just listened to the creak of the stairs and the muffled sound of the attic door opening, then closing. A pause. Footsteps coming back.

"It's done," Caleb said, brushing dust off his hands. "He's back in the chest."

Emma didn't smile. She got up and went to take a shower.

✖✖✖✖✖✖

THE BABY SHOWER WAS SMALL—INTIMATE, low-key, just the way Emma had wanted it. Five women she still trusted. Her sister-in-law Jordan brought lemon bars in a pastel pink tin. Marcy, from book club, wore bright red lipstick and held court like she always did. Her old coworkers Sarah and Janine arrived together, each toting a gift bag and a bottle of sparkling apple cider. And Laurel, her former roommate, came late, flustered but glowing, with a bag of gently used baby books from her own kids.

The kitchen was filled with warmth: the smell of buttercream and brewed coffee, the flick of candles on the counter, the hum of happy voices. Someone brought onesie-shaped sugar cookies. Finger sandwiches were stacked on a tiered tray. The banner that read "Welcome Baby Otis" drooped slightly on one end, but no one cared.

Presents piled on the coffee table—soft things and sweet things and practical things. Emma sat in the center of it all, cheeks flushed, one hand resting absently on her belly.

"I'm serious," Marcy said, holding out a tiny pair of socks. "If this kid doesn't come out with an Instagram account, you're doing it wrong."

Emma laughed, and the room laughed with her. For a while, everything felt almost normal.

She opened a sleek mint-green box tied with silver ribbon and pulled out a brand-new video baby monitor. "Oh wow."

"Top of the line," Marcy said. "Motion detection, night vision, sound alerts. It practically parents for you."

Emma smiled. "We hadn't gotten one yet. This is perfect."

As they moved on to cupcakes, Marcy snapped a group photo—everyone bunched together, half-laughing, pink punch in hand. A few minutes later, she let out a small sound as she scrolled through her camera roll.

"Um, who's that behind the curtain?"

Emma leaned over.

Behind the sheer sliding door curtain, barely visible in the far edge of the frame, stood a shadow

—rounded, upright, wrong. Not a person. Not exactly. It had the shape of something stuffed, but somehow poised.

"Probably just a reflection of something outside," Emma said quickly, forcing a breathy laugh. "It's a mess out there. We still haven't organized the patio."

No one questioned her. Marcy shrugged and kept scrolling. The others went back to their cupcakes.

But Emma didn't stop watching the curtain for the rest of the afternoon.

✗✗✗✗✗✗

THAT NIGHT, the house was too quiet. The air felt unusually still after the motion and color of the day.

Emma and Caleb stood in the nursery, assembling the last of the gifts. Diapers stacked in neat towers. A cozy blanket folded over the crib rail. The monitor box sat unopened on the changing table.

"I figured we'd do this before we're too tired to care," Caleb said, holding up the camera.

Emma nodded and took the receiver, plugging it in beside her side of the bed. The screen lit up—a static-filled grayscale of the nursery. Crib, chair, shelves. All perfectly still.

Caleb mounted the camera above the crib and

adjusted it twice. "It'll pick up sound from the hallway too."

The nursery in black and white looked different. Less cheerful. Like something out of time.

"You good?" he asked, dusting his hands.

"Yeah," Emma said. But she didn't look away from the screen.

They climbed into bed, the monitor humming quietly between them. Caleb scrolled his phone for a while before rolling over and muttering, "Love you, Em."

"Love you too."

She lay there long after he drifted off, eyes on the screen.

The image didn't change.

But she kept watching, waiting for something to move in the margins.

And just once—just briefly—she thought she saw the shadow of the rocking chair tilt, ever so slightly, forward.

That's enough of that. All you're doing is freaking yourself out.

She rolled to face the other way and shifted under the covers, unable to get comfortable. Every time she closed her eyes, the image of the bear in her arms returned—too vivid, too real to dismiss as a dream. The way it had been tucked against her, like it had crawled there on its own and waited for her to wake up.

Emma rolled back over and glanced at the monitor again. The nursery looked quiet. The tiny mobile above the crib—clouds and stars in pale felt—cast faint shadows along the wall. But something about it made her skin itch.

She got out of bed.

Caleb stirred slightly but didn't wake as she padded down the hallway barefoot. The floorboards were cool under her feet. The door to the nursery creaked faintly when she pushed it open.

Nothing had changed. Not really.

She walked to the crib, pressed a hand gently against the mattress, then touched the folded blanket on the rail. Still neat. Still soft. Still untouched.

The chair sat where it always had. No bear. Everything as it should be.

She closed the door behind her and went back to bed. She curled under the covers but left the monitor's screen on. She watched it until her vision went fuzzy. Until the contrast of black and white began to blur and swim.

She eventually drifted off to sleep. But it wasn't peaceful.

THIS TIME she stood in the nursery—only it wasn't the nursery. It was older, grayer, the paint peeling and the floor warped. The mobile was still above the crib, but the shapes had changed. No more clouds. Just wire, twisted and rusted.

The boy was there again.

He stood near the wall, his small frame silhouetted by a shaft of impossible light coming from nowhere. He clutched Cubby tightly, tighter than before, like the bear was the only thing holding him together.

When he turned his head, Emma saw his eyes.

Wide. Hollow. Wet with panic.

"Don't let him out," he whispered.

And then the light went out.

✖✖✖✖✖✖

EMMA SAT UP IN BED, heart racing.

The monitor still showed the nursery, still unchanged.

Still empty.

She leaned closer, nose almost to the screen. Looked at every corner. She didn't know what she expected to see, but she couldn't shake the feeling she'd already missed it.

Nothing moved.

She sank back onto the pillow but couldn't close

her eyes again. Somewhere inside her, something had shifted. Like the edge of her world had curled just slightly, revealing something darker underneath.

The bear wasn't just strange anymore. It was watching.

✖✖✖✖✖✖

1967

TWELVE-YEAR-OLD RICHARD RODE his bike home after school, Tommy trailing behind. The younger boy, maybe ten or eleven, grinned with the open eagerness of a kid who thought it was cool to have an older friend who was going to show him something top secret. They dumped their bikes on the side of the house.

"Thanks again for asking me to come over for your birthday!" Tommy panted. "What kind of cupcakes did you say your mom made?"

"Uhhh. Not sure. But let me show what I found in the barn first. I'm pretty sure it's my present."

"I hope it's a new bike. Yours is really beat up."

Richard's eyes narrowed. "Just come see!"

The barn loomed, its boards weathered but strong. Richard led them through the doors, pulling them shut behind with a low groan of old hinges. He slid the bolt into place with a click that echoed like a verdict.

"Why'd you do that? It's dark in here!"

Dust drifted in sunlit beams. The air was thick and cloying with hay and dirt and rust.

Cubby sat upright against a wooden post, pristine amid the grime. Not a speck of dust on him. The school, and his mom, had finally forced him to leave Cubby at home. It wasn't *normal* for a boy his age to bring his bear to school they had said.

"Whoa," Tommy said. "A teddy bear? That's not a cool present."

"Yeah, you got a problem with it?" Richard moved across the barn. He stepped behind a stack of hay bales and came back holding a shovel.

Tommy's smile faltered. "Hey, what's that for?"

Richard didn't reply.

"Richard?"

He raised the shovel.

The blow landed with a sickening thud. Tommy dropped like a rag doll. One hit. That's all it took. His body twitched once, then stilled.

Richard breathed evenly, eyes blank. He dragged the boy's body across the dirt floor, then began digging. The sound of the shovel biting earth was rhythmic. Purposeful. Efficient.

No rage. No panic. Just work.

When the shallow grave was done, he lowered

the body in and covered it carefully. He dusted off his hands.

Then he picked up Cubby and posed him beside Tommy's body, adjusting the bear's arms and tilting his head just so. From his coat pocket, Richard retrieved a Polaroid camera. He'd asked his mom for one, but of course she wouldn't buy it from him. So, he had stolen one from Sears. He clicked the shutter and waited for the photo to develop, watching as the image slowly appeared. Cubby beside the lifeless body, both still, both eternal.

He placed the photograph into his back pocket to take back to his room.

Finally, he picked Cubby up again and stepped outside. The sunlight touched its glass eyes, and for a moment, they sparkled.

"Happy birthday, Cubby. This is the best one yet!"

He closed the barn door and slid the bolt shut behind him.

CHAPTER
FIVE

"I think the Halloween stuff is up here," Caleb said, already halfway up the attic steps.

Emma followed slowly, one hand resting on her belly. "We really should've labeled the boxes better."

"I did," Caleb said. "You're the one who decided 'Kitchen-ish' was a valid category."

She smirked, ducking under a beam as she stepped into the attic. The overhead light flickered once before settling into a dull glow. Dust motes swirled in the air. The familiar scent of wood, paper, and insulation filled the space.

They split up, checking boxes and lifting lids, moving slowly.

Emma veered toward the back corner, near the old cedar chest where she'd found Cubby. That's when she noticed something different.

The door.

The one that had always been locked—small, unassuming, painted the same dull color as the attic wall—was cracked open.

"Caleb," she called.

He turned. "What?"

She pointed. "That door. It's open."

He frowned. "Was it like that before?"

"No," she said. "I've checked it. It was locked tight. We never found the key, did we?"

"What the hell?"

Emma shrugged, and they exchanged a glance. Neither of them moved at first. Then Caleb stepped forward and nudged the door wider. The hinges creaked, the sound loud in the stillness.

Beyond it was a room neither had seen before.

It was small—low ceilinged, narrow, more like a crawl space than a proper room, but just tall enough to stand in. The air inside was colder, stale in a way that made Emma's skin prickle.

Caleb reached for the pull-chain light just inside the doorway. It clicked, but nothing happened. No bulb. Just darkness.

Emma stepped forward anyway, phone flashlight raised.

The beam cut through the gloom, revealing a space that made both of them stop short.

A child-sized twin bed sat along the far wall, low to the ground, with a sunken mattress stained dark in the center. No pillow. No blankets. Just the mattress, sagging, warped by time.

Beside it, a small wooden table leaned slightly to the left. The top was faded yellow; edges blistered with old burn marks that curled inward like fingers. One of the table legs had a splintered crack running through it.

On the floor, broken and melted toys lay scattered. Dolls missing limbs, a plastic truck with warped wheels, a stuffed rabbit slumped in the corner, its fur melted into hard clumps. It smelled faintly of scorched plastic.

Emma's breath caught.

The floor was stained. The walls were cracked and covered in wallpaper that hung in long, curling strips, revealing the plaster beneath. And on nearly every exposed surface were crude stick-figure drawings. Dozens of them. Scrawled in black crayon, red crayon, something that might've been charcoal. Some had no heads. Others were bleeding from jagged necks or stomachs. A few were buried underground, with only hands or eyes above the soil, marked with little red Xs.

One figure appeared again and again—larger than the others, holding something round in its arms. In one version, the thing in its arms was a stuffed bear.

Emma stepped closer. Her light caught on something shiny, reflecting back. A broken picture frame was nailed to the wall, glass cracked and empty.

The silence in the room felt loaded now, not empty but crowded—with impressions, maybe, or memory.

"Jesus," Caleb whispered beside her.

She didn't respond.

Emma's throat felt tight. "We shouldn't be in here."

Caleb gave one small nod. "Let's go."

Something on the floor caught Caleb's attention as they were leaving the room, but Emma didn't pause long enough to see what it was. Caleb closed the door behind him, but it didn't click shut. Neither of them tried to fix it.

�✗✗✗✗✗

THAT NIGHT, Emma barely slept.

She lay in bed watching the baby monitor, the grainy black-and-white feed showing the quiet nursery. The crib. The rocking chair. The shelves. All still.

At some point, she drifted off. Her dreams came in flashes—peeling wallpaper, the warped bed, dolls whispering without mouths. A hallway that stretched on forever. A handprint on the inside of the crib.

❌❌❌❌❌❌

IN THE EARLY light of morning, she padded into the hallway toward the kitchen—and stopped cold.

The nursery was open. Cubby was in the crib.

Not tossed in, not slumped. Placed.

He lay tucked against the tiny pillow, head resting gently to one side, glassy eyes reflecting the sunlight.

Emma didn't move.

Something was different. No blue bow.

A moment later, Caleb appeared beside her, half-dressed and bleary-eyed. His face changed the moment he saw the bear.

"Nope," he said. "Nope. We are *not* doing this today."

He crossed the room and picked Cubby up, inspecting the seams, the back of the neck, inside the tag.

"The bow's gone," he muttered, and put him back in the crib.

Emma only nodded.

It wasn't until later, after breakfast, when Caleb reached down to clip Daisy's leash to her collar, that he froze.

Emma saw it too.

The bow.

Blue velvet. Neatly tied. Dangling just below the clasp of Daisy's collar.

Emma crouched beside her. She reached out, untied it, and threw it in the trash.

They didn't speak.

Caleb leashed Daisy up and walked her out the front door. Emma didn't follow. She wandered down the hall, drawn back toward the nursery like gravity had shifted.

Cubby was still in the crib.

He hadn't moved—but something about him felt different now, like he wasn't just *placed* there, but *waiting*. His glass eyes caught the morning light in two sharp glints. The absence of the bow made his small, round body look even more stark. Exposed.

She stepped closer, slow, her footsteps soft against the floor.

The room felt colder. Not a draft—just a drop in weight, a pressure in the air that made her ears ring faintly. Like a storm was building inside the walls.

A faint hum filled the space. She looked around, then realized it was the monitor. Nothing unusual. Just its gentle, mechanical buzz. But for a moment, it almost sounded like breathing.

She glanced at the bear again.

The crib mattress was slightly indented beneath his body.

Emma reached out, then stopped herself. She wasn't sure what she had meant to do—touch him? Move him?

She pulled her hand back.

Instead, she sat in the rocking chair and watched.

The longer she sat, the more the quiet pressed in. Dust hung in the light from the window, drifting in slow spirals. Somewhere in the walls, the house gave a faint groan—a settling beam or a shifting pipe—but it sounded too much like a sigh.

She folded her arms across her chest and rocked gently, letting the motion lull her nerves. But her eyes never left the crib.

She didn't know how long she sat there. Ten minutes. Maybe more. Eventually, the front door opened and closed again. Daisy's nails clicked across the floor. Caleb called her name once, then again.

She rose slowly from the rocking chair, knees stiff. The hum of the monitor faded into the background, replaced by the sound of Daisy's collar jingling down the hall. She crossed to the crib. Cubby lay just as she'd left him—still, blank, harmless in the way a toy should be.

But it was the stillness that unsettled her now.

She reached down and turned him around so he wasn't looking at her any more, as if that might prove something. The bear's fur was warm. Too warm. Not like sun-through-the-window warm. Something else.

Alive wasn't the word.

She jerked her hand back and turned toward the door. Caleb was calling her again. Emma left the nursery without looking back, but she didn't close the door. She paused in the hallway, listening. Nothing.

She forced her feet to move, turning toward the kitchen, letting the light and sound of morning reorient her. But as she walked, something tugged at her attention. Not a sound. Not a movement. Just a pull, gentle and magnetic, from the room behind her.

She didn't give in to it.

Instead, she took her place at the counter, lifted her tea, and smiled faintly as Caleb stepped into the kitchen with Daisy trotting behind him, leash slack in his hand.

"You okay?" he asked.

Emma nodded.

She reheated her tea in the microwave, then took a sip, the warmth grounding her for a moment. Caleb moved around the kitchen, rinsing Daisy's water bowl, humming something tuneless under his breath. The normalcy of it made her stomach tighten.

She glanced toward the hallway. The nursery

door stood half open, just as she'd left it. She told herself not to check. Told herself it was fine.

Instead, she moved to the sink and washed her cup, watching the soap swirl and vanish. When she dried her hands, her fingers were shaking.

Caleb didn't notice. It was like he had already forgotten everything that happened last night and this morning. He kissed her on the cheek as he passed, mumbling something about "putting the goddamn bear back in the attic" and needing to finish the shelves in the laundry room.

❌❌❌❌❌❌

CALEB STOOD at the base of the attic stairs; Cubby clutched awkwardly under one arm like an unruly child. The bear's fur was soft, its glass eyes dull in the low light—except, in certain angles, they almost looked . . . real. Watching every move.

He shook the thought off.

"It's just a toy," he muttered to himself. "Old house, drafty attic, gravity, the dog. That's all. That has to be all."

The wooden steps creaked as he climbed, each one groaning louder than the last. The air up here was heavier, thick with insulation dust and something else—like mildew and old paper. The bulb overhead buzzed dimly, casting shadows that leaned the wrong way.

Caleb crouched beside the cedar chest, opened the lid, and placed the bear inside. He reached to close it, hesitated, then picked the bear up again. For a moment, he looked into its shiny glass eyes.

"Stay there, you little shit," he said, only half-joking, and set the bear down once more before closing the chest.

He turned to leave, but something made him glance back. Then he remembered the notebook he had seen in the strange room and went to retrieve it.

As he shut the attic door behind him, he slid the latch closed. Not to keep anyone out.

To keep it in.

1970

RICHARD STOOD in the center of his room in the attic of the house, a place no one visited anymore. Cracks ran down the walls like spiderwebs, and the wallpaper peeled in long, curling sheets. He moved with mechanical precision, arranging fifteen half-burnt candles in a perfect circle around a rickety card table. Each flickering flame threw long, jittery shadows that seemed to dance just out of sync with the light.

Cubby sat at the head of the table on a cheap metal folding chair, his blue velvet bow perfectly straight. His black glass eyes gleamed, catching the candlelight in a way that made them seem almost wet—alive.

Across from the bear sat a young boy—thirteen, maybe fourteen—tied tightly to a dining chair. The rope bit into his arms and legs. A rag, grey with grime, was jammed into his mouth. His face was blotchy with tears, and he wheezed through his nose in panicked bursts.

Richard stepped back and surveyed the scene. He nodded, as if satisfied with the symmetry. Cupcakes he'd made himself. The icing was clumsy, an uneven dome of white sugar and rainbow sprinkles. Party hats, blue with yellow stars. Then, humming softly, he picked up the candles, placed one in each of the three cupcakes and lit them.

"Happy birthday to us," Richard whispered, his voice full of an emotion that didn't match the scene. His gaze fell lovingly on Cubby.

He placed a cupcake in front of Cubby first, setting the plate as if the bear might actually eat it. Then he turned to the boy.

"You're lucky, you know," he said, crouching in front of the child. "You're sooo lucky to be here,

Sean. Me and Cubby have the same birthday, and I've never had a real party before."

Richard placed a party hat on Sean's head. The boy screeched behind the gag, eyes bulging with terror.

"You know what the head shrinker doctor said about me?" Richard asked as he arranged the party hats on the table. His voice was almost conversational.

The boy tied to the chair whimpered.

"He said I had . . . detachment issues. That I couldn't form normal bonds, whatever that means. I was projecting emotional stability onto an object." Richard chuckled to himself. "Stupid school made me see this man every week for a year. But he said if I could be normal and make real friends I could stop coming to his stupid office. So, you and me became friends. Well, not *real* friends. You've been a real asshole, you know? You made fun of me and Cubby until I stopped bringing him to school a couple years ago. But Cubby said I should invite you because that's what he wanted for his birthday!"

Richard tilted his head, listening. Then, as if the boy had spoken words, he smiled. "I know. You're scared. I'm scared too. But Cubby wants something really special for his birthday."

The knife gleamed as he stood. The flickering light caught on its blade. He raised it slowly—not like an attack, but like an offering.

Then he brought it down.

There was no struggle. No screaming, only the sound of something wet and final. Blood splattered across the floor and speckled the edges of the cupcakes. The body slumped forward, face-first into the table, ropes tightening as it fell.

Richard stood over the scene for a long moment, breathing through his nose. The scent rose up to meet him—warm, metallic, and thick. It coated the back of his throat, copper, salt and something faintly sweet, like pennies dropped in a sun-baked pool of sugar water. His expression never changed. Calm. Almost serene. When the stillness settled, he wiped the knife clean and placed it carefully on the windowsill. He turned to Cubby.

"I'm so glad you told me to invite him," he said softly, and took a bite of a cupcake. "Happy birthday, Cubby."

From a battered dresser in the corner, he pulled out a Polaroid camera. He scooted the chair against the wall, lifting the boy's head upright and tilting it to rest on the wall, blood still dripping from his throat. Then he posed Cubby beside the corpse, placing the bear on the boy's shoulder.

He stepped back, framed the shot, and clicked the shutter.

The photo ejected with a mechanical whir. Richard held it as the image developed—first ghostly shapes, then color and detail. Sean, lifeless and bloodied. Cubby, perfect and untouched.

Richard slipped the photo into a notebook on the dresser, beneath a stack of similar ones. A collection.

Then, with slow, reverent movements, he blew out each candle. One by one.

He scooped Cubby up and hugged him then dragged Sean out to the barn to join his birthday collection.

CHAPTER
SIX

Emma watched Caleb disappear up the stairs with Cubby dangling under one arm like an oversized prop. He didn't speak on his way down.

When he returned, he had something tucked under his arm—a thin, battered notebook with a black-and-white marbled cover.

"Forget the laundry room," he said. "You need to see this."

Emma looked up from the kitchen table, where she'd been folding towels with more focus than necessary.

"I meant to grab it yesterday," Caleb added. "I saw it on the floor in that little room. Near the bed. I didn't want to stay in there any longer than we had to."

He placed the notebook on the table between them.

It was an old composition book, the kind they used in grade school. The cover was worn to the edges, water-stained and slightly bowed. Emma reached out and flipped it open.

Inside, the pages were filled with uneven, child-like handwriting. Some letters backward. Some words repeated. No dates.

She read aloud the first few lines she came to.

"Cubby don't hit me."

A few pages later:

"She was mad I was talking to him again."

Another, written over and over like a mantra:

"Billy said Cubby is for babies. He's wrong. He's wrong. He's wrong."

Another page toward the back:

"Stupid ferret. I hate him. I hate mom."

Emma flipped through the pages, taking each one in. The ink changed colors. Some entries were barely legible. One page was covered in angry scribbles, as if the writer had tried to black out the words. Others were spaced strangely, with letters fading mid-sentence like the pencil had been taken away.

Most ended the same way: a crude drawing of a teddy bear.

She stared at one of the bears—its circle face filled in with heavy, dark pressure. Tiny black dots for eyes, a jagged triangle for a mouth. The shape of it was unmistakable. Her stomach turned.

Her throat felt dry. She hadn't blinked in what felt like minutes. She wanted to close the book, but something in her refused—like turning away would be an invitation.

Emma closed the book. Her fingers lingered on the cover.

"Who would write this?" she breathed.

Caleb shook his head. "A really disturbed kid. Someone who lived here?"

"Did . . . do you . . . was Cubby his?"

They sat with that for a long moment, both of them staring at the notebook like it might keep writing.

"It's . . . it's like Cubby was real to him. Not just a toy. More than that."

"Sounds like he was alone," Caleb said. "A lot."

Emma looked down again. "He didn't have anybody but the bear."

The silence stretched. The notebook made her uncomfortable. A sense of impropriety washed over her as their voices drowned out the notebook's quiet presence. She pushed it toward the corner of the table, as though giving it space might lessen the weight in the room.

Caleb didn't touch it. He didn't even look at her. It was like they were both pretending the thing between them was just paper and ink—not something leftover and watching.

"We should have left it up there," she said.

That night, neither of them said much. The notebook sat closed on the kitchen counter, just far enough from the stove to avoid splashes of boiling water.

Emma caught herself glancing at it while chopping vegetables, like it might move. She hated how aware she was of it—how her body wanted to keep turning toward it, like it was a person who might be staring.

After dinner, they went through the motions—dishes, teeth brushed, lights dimmed. Caleb checked the locks. Emma straightened a basket of folded onesies, mostly to keep her hands busy. The house was quiet, save for the distant hum of the fridge and the creak of floorboards as they moved from room to room.

When Caleb kissed her cheek goodnight, Emma jumped.

"Didn't mean to sneak up," he said softly.

"It's okay," she whispered. But her skin prickled where he'd touched her.

She paused at the nursery door, fingers brushing the frame. The crib looked undisturbed. The air in the room felt normal. But she still backed out slowly and shut the door like something might follow.

She went back to the monitor and sat on the edge of the bed. The image blinked to life.

Crib. Shelves. Rocking chair.

Cubby was not there.

Then the monitor flickered.

The screen went white, then black, then returned to normal.

But in that two-second interruption, Emma could've sworn she saw Cubby in the chair.

She saw his eyes close. Then open again.

A blink.

She stiffened.

"What?" Caleb said from behind her, already pulling back the sheets.

"Nothing," she said quickly. "It glitched."

"You okay?"

Emma didn't hesitate. "No," she said. Her voice was quiet, but sharp. "I saw something."

Caleb blinked, surprised. "What do you mean?"

She grabbed her phone, opened the baby monitor app, and navigated to the cloud storage. Her fingers moved quickly, swiping back through the most recent recordings.

"There," she said, tapping to play. "Watch right after the flicker."

They both stared at the screen as the footage rolled: grayscale image, then static, then the room again.

Caleb leaned closer. "It's just static."

"No," Emma said. "That's not what I saw. Go back."

She scrubbed backward and replayed the same few seconds again. The monitor flashed white, then black—and in that half-second of distortion, something moved.

A blur. A shape. Nothing definitive.

But Emma saw it again: the outline in the chair. And the eyes. Closing.

Then open.

A blink.

"There," she said, almost whispering. "You saw it that time, right?"

Caleb exhaled. "I saw . . . maybe something. It was fast."

"I saw him. In the chair. He blinked. I'm not making it up."

"I didn't say you were, Em."

He reached out and squeezed her hand—just once, quick. A peace offering.

She sat with the phone still glowing in her palm, thumb hovering over the pause button. Her eyes flicked to the timestamp. 1:13 a.m.

She hit rewind again. One second. Two.

There: static, then clarity. Empty chair this time.

She let the video play out another minute. Nothing moved.

Finally, she closed the app, set the phone on the nightstand, and turned off the lamp.

She lay beside Caleb in the dark, listening to his breathing even out.

How can he be so nonchalant about all of—

She never got to finish her thought.

1973

RICHARD SET a beer down in front of her, careful not to let it slosh over the rim of the glass. He'd stolen it from the fridge while his mother was passed out on the couch with daytime television reruns blaring. *That bitch will never notice, she never does.* She hadn't said a word to him that morning. She never did, not ever.

Leah smiled, twisting a lock of hair around her finger. "Fancy," she teased. "Thanks for the invite. Sorry I didn't get you anything."

She didn't know she was the gift.

Her name was Leah. She was seventeen and worked the register at the convenience store. She always chewed strawberry gum. Wore cheap bracelets that jingled. Once, she told him he had nice eyes.

That was enough.

He started visiting more often. Showed up right

before closing when the store was empty. He never said much. Just bought a soda or a candy bar and lingered. He waited for her to smile.

Eventually, she did. Again. And again.

She liked the attention. Or maybe she liked the idea of being liked.

Last week, he told her it was almost his birthday.

"Oh, yeah?" she'd said, gum snapping between her teeth. "Doing anything special?"

"Party," he'd said. "Small. Just a few people. You should come. I'll have beer."

She laughed, light and surprised. "Sure. Why not."

She thought he was weird. But she wasn't going to turn down free beer.

XXXXXXX

"You really listen," she said now, her voice softer, a little hazy. "Not many guys do that. Most just wanna talk about themselves."

Richard smiled, small and stiff. He sat opposite her in the living room, legs crossed, hands resting on his knees. The couch groaned when she shifted. His heart beat slow and even.

He'd planned this for weeks.

Behind her, Cubby sat upright in the armchair, bow

freshly tied, fur brushed smooth. Richard had placed him there himself. The two candles lit on the table cast flickering shadows across the bear's glass eyes.

This time, he only lit two candles.

One for him.

One for Cubby.

She didn't matter.

Leah sipped the beer. "Tastes kinda funny."

"It's a German import," he said. "Rare. Thought you'd like it."

She blinked slowly. "Kinda bitter, but . . . it's fine."

She looked around. "So, when's everyone else getting here?"

Richard paused. "They're running late."

She nodded, but her head swayed. Her eyelids were getting heavier. "You sure they're even coming?" she mumbled.

"They said they would," he said, watching her closely.

He tilted his head. "Are you feeling okay?"

"Yeah, just dizzy." She laughed, sluggish. "Think I drank too fast."

"Maybe." He leaned forward, elbows on his knees. "You're beautiful. Not like the others."

She didn't answer. Her eyes fluttered closed, then opened halfway. Then closed again.

Moments later, her body sagged against the

cushions. The bottle slipped from her hand and clinked against the hardwood.

Richard caught her before she could fall. Lowered her gently to the green rug with the knotted fringe. She was light. Her breathing was slow and even.

He brushed the hair back from her forehead.

"Cubby," he said softly. "She's a good one. She was kind to me. Are you sure this is what you want? You're still my best friend. But I like her." He paused to look at the bear. "Ok, I know what the blink means."

He stood and walked to the kitchen. The drawer under the sink opened with a familiar creak. Inside: the knife, wrapped in an old dish towel, polished that morning. Not because it needed to be sharp— but because it should be clean. Ritual deserved respect.

When he returned, the room had stilled. The candles flickered. Cubby watched from his chair.

Richard knelt beside Leah and unfolded the blade beside her.

He touched her shoulder gently.

This part wasn't about anger. It wasn't even about her.

This was about the day.

He didn't speak while he worked. He moved carefully, methodically. Each cut placed with the precision of someone who'd studied, someone who cared.

The blood came fast, dark and warm. It spread over the rug like ink, pooling beneath her back. When it was finished, he sat back on his heels, breathing slowly. He took the damp cloth he'd prepared and cleaned her face. Closed her eyes. Smoothed her hair again. Arranged her hands neatly at her sides. She looked peaceful now. Almost grateful. He picked up Cubby and placed the bear at her side.

"Look," he whispered. "Look what I got for you."

He adjusted the bow again. Then he stood and retrieved the camera. The Polaroid was already loaded. He crouched low, framed the shot, and clicked the shutter.

Flash.

The light burst across the room. Then darkness swallowed it whole. He waited while the image developed in his hand. The picture came in slowly. A girl on a rug. A bear beside her. Candles glowing behind them. *It's beautiful.*

"Cubby," he said. "She's special, I got her just for you. Happy birthday."

The bear blinked once in response and Richard knew he was pleased.

Richard smiled.

CHAPTER
SEVEN

How can he be so nonchalant about all of—
Emma gasped and doubled forward. A sudden pressure tightened in her abdomen, and then warmth spread between her legs.

"Caleb," she said sharply. "My water just broke."

He sat up immediately. "What? Are you sure?"

She looked at him, wide-eyed, then down to where she was sitting. "I'm very sure."

Everything after that moved in a blur. Caleb grabbed the hospital bag. Emma changed clothes. The drive was faster than either of them remembered. Traffic didn't exist. The world seemed to clear a path for them.

She tried to stay calm, to focus on her breathing, but her mind kept returning to the bear. Cubby. Not fear, exactly—more like a shadow of knowing, like something had shifted, and nothing was going to shift back.

Time folded around her. One minute she was walking into the hospital. The next she was gripping Caleb's hand, muscles tightening, someone telling her to push. A voice. Hers? Someone else's? She wasn't sure. Everything blurred at the edges, raw and bright and surreal. At one point, she thought she heard someone whisper her name, but when she looked, no one was near her head. She thought she saw a shadow in the light above her. But there was no time to ask. The next contraction crashed over her like a wave.

And then, for just a second—between the peaks of pain, between the noise and breath and push—she swore she saw him.

Cubby.

Just a glimpse. In the corner of the room. A soft brown shape, glassy eyes catching the light.

And then he was gone.

No one else reacted. No one else saw. Maybe it hadn't happened at all.

But then came the crying. Sharp and small and immediate.

Otis.

The nurse placed him on her chest, and Emma wept. Caleb was crying too, brushing hair from her face, telling her she'd done amazing, that their son was perfect, that he loved her.

She held Otis and didn't look at the corners again.

✗✗✗✗✗✗✗

THE HOSPITAL ROOM was too quiet in the early morning. Emma woke to the sounds of nurses in the hallway and the distant beep of another monitor down the hall. Her body ached, her skin felt stretched, but Otis was sleeping soundly beside her in a clear bassinet.

She smiled, dazed with the surreal weight of it all. The window let in early light, pale and blue. She reached out to touch the edge of the bassinet, needing that contact to prove everything was real.

Then she saw it.

A flash of color against white hospital linens. Something tucked just beneath Otis's swaddled feet.

Emma leaned over, heart skipping.

The blue velvet bow.

Cubby's bow. The one they threw away.

No bear—just the ribbon, neatly tied, pristine. Like a gift.

Her hands hovered above it. She didn't want to touch it. She looked at the door. Still closed. The curtain undisturbed. No one else had come in.

She picked it up carefully, held it like it might bite.

"Caleb," she whispered, her voice barely rising.

He stirred in the vinyl recliner, rubbing his eyes. "What's wrong?"

She turned the bow toward him. "It was in his crib."

Caleb blinked slowly, then sat up. "Is this a joke?"

She shook her head.

Neither of them said anything else. Caleb rose, checked the hallway, then sat back down and stared at the floor.

They didn't report it. What would they say? We're so sorry but we think a haunted teddy bear left our baby a gift?

She kept the bow. Folded it in a tissue and buried it deep in the diaper bag, unsure if she was hiding it from him or herself. She left it there for about an hour, but she couldn't stand it anymore. When she was alone, she got up and stuffed it in the red sharps box on the wall.

🧸🧸🧸🧸🧸🧸

WHEN THEY CAME HOME, everything was as they'd left it.

The nursery still smelled like fresh paint and baby lotion. Caleb carried Otis in, placed the car seat gently by the crib. Daisy hovered nearby, tail wagging cautiously. She sniffed the baby, then wandered out without a sound.

Emma moved through the house in a soft daze, half-tired, half-euphoric. She kissed Caleb in the hallway. She cried over a freezer meal. They napped in shifts. They took pictures. Otis's tiny body curled up perfectly on her chest. Everything felt raw and real and wonderful and impossible to explain.

She found herself narrating everything she did to Otis as if he understood. "We're folding laundry now," she'd whisper. "You hate diaper changes, but we're going to get through this together." His eyes would blink; his tiny mouth would pucker like he was listening and wanted to respond. It soothed her more than it soothed him.

At night, Emma sometimes caught herself standing in the hallway just outside the nursery, holding her breath. Not for fear—more like a habit. Waiting for something she couldn't name. Then Otis would whimper or sigh in his sleep, and she'd step inside and shush him gently, grounding herself in the moment.

Weeks passed. The baby grew like a weed. Emma's body healed. Caleb returned to his work duties. Life settled.

Until the morning she found Cubby in the nursery.

He was sitting in the rocking chair. His onyx gaze directed toward the crib.

The blue velvet bow was tied neatly back around his neck. Emma stood in the doorway, paralyzed. She hadn't seen that bow since the hospital. She called for Caleb. He came, still holding a coffee mug, then stopped dead when he saw the bear.

"I didn't bring him down," he said immediately.

"Neither did I."

They stared at Cubby like he might move. He didn't.

Caleb picked him up and carried him straight to the attic. This time, he locked the door behind him and moved a chair in front of it.

They didn't speak of it. Not that day. Not the next. That night, Emma lay awake, watching the ceiling shift with headlights from passing cars. She thought she heard something in the attic. A thud. Then a dragging noise. But when she nudged Caleb awake, he said it was just the house settling. Emma didn't believe him. Not really. But she didn't want to go up there alone. Not again.

🧸🧸🧸🧸🧸🧸

THREE DAYS LATER, she woke up to Otis babbling softly on the monitor. A sleepy, rhythmic coo. Normal.

She got up and walked down the hall in the early light. The house creaked around her like it always did. The floor cooled her bare feet. The baby's noise got louder.

And then she reached the nursery.

Cubby was back.

Same chair. Same position. Same bow.

Exactly where he wanted to be.

Emma didn't scream. She didn't wake Caleb. She walked in and gently picked Otis up out of the crib, rocking him against her shoulder as she scurried out of the room. She didn't look at the bear.

Not yet. She couldn't.

She would wait until the baby was safe. Until Caleb was awake. Until it was light outside.

Then they'd move Cubby again. Not because it would work. But because it was the only thing they knew how to do.

And for now, that would have to be enough.

1977

RICHARD SPENT his twenty-second birthday slicing shrink wrap off pallets of canned creamed corn.

No cake. No card. Just the hum of fluorescent lights and the drone of the radio station playing crappy music through the grocery store intercom.

Marlene offered him a smile in the break room. "Hey, Rick. You doing anything tonight, birthday boy?"

He shrugged. "Probably not." He hated it when she called him Rick.

She didn't press. Just went back to eating her crackers and scribbling in a little notebook. He watched her chew. Heard the way her jaw clicked. It set his teeth on edge.

Later, at the register, he heard her laugh with Jimmy—the seventeen-year-old bag boy who smelled like deodorant and cheap aftershave. Heard Jimmy say, "I think Richard talks to the soup cans when no one's around."

He heard her laugh again.

And Cubby heard it too.

That night, the parking lot was slick from a light drizzle. Marlene left through the back like always, keys jangling in her hand. Richard stood beside his beat-up Bronco, hood propped up.

"Hey," he called. "Can you give me a hand? Battery's acting weird."

She sighed but walked over. "Sure. What do you need?"

"Just hold this," he said, handing her a flashlight.

When she leaned over, he struck.

Fast. Blunt force. The tire iron landed with a wet crack. Once. Twice. Three times.

She crumpled onto the gravel.

Richard dragged her body into the back seat of his car. Her breath came in shallow, ragged pulls. She was still alive.

He sat beside her, lifted Cubby from the glove box, and tucked the bear gently into her arms.

"You shouldn't have laughed," he whispered. "Today's our birthday. You were supposed to be nice to me."

She blinked slowly, lips parting. Tried to speak.

He shushed her. "I hate it when you call me Rick. And Cubby hates it when people laugh at me."

Then he wrapped her scarf tight around her throat and pulled until she stopped moving.

When he got home, he took her to the barn to bury her with the others. But not before snapping a picture of Cubby with his birthday gift. Her name—MARLENE—in shaky blue ink across the bottom.

He added it to the others.

CHAPTER
EIGHT

At first, it was just one thing.

A small rattle Emma didn't remember buying—wooden, old-fashioned, painted with faded red stars. She found it on the edge of the changing table one morning, nestled between folded burp cloths. It was clean. Polished, even. The kind of toy that felt older than it looked.

She assumed it was a gift from someone, maybe something left at the door that Caleb forgot to tell her about. Or maybe something from Caleb's parents. They were always dropping things off without warning. But when she asked him about it, he only frowned.

"I didn't get it," he said. "You sure it's not from the baby shower?"

Emma shook her head slowly. "It wasn't here yesterday." She tucked it away in a dresser drawer.

They let it go. Their constant new-parent sleep deprivation made it easy to ignore oddities.

Then came the toy car.

A single car. Small, metal. Dull blue with chipped paint and patina. It was placed neatly on the windowsill beside the crib, just under the blackout curtain. Emma stood staring at it for a full minute before reaching out to touch it. Cold. Heavy. Worn smooth with time.

"Did you put this here?" she asked Caleb later, holding it out on her palm.

He looked at her like she was handing him a dead bird. "Where'd you get that?"

"In the nursery. On the windowsill."

He shook his head slowly. "That's not from me. He's too little for those kinds of toys."

"Obviously, but . . . I'm getting rid of it."

It didn't stop.

Every few days they found something new, a single item, placed somewhere in the nursery.

A yellowed pacifier, the kind with the big rubber nipple that had gone out of production decades ago for safety reasons. A cloth doll with no face, its threadbare dress faded to near-white. A sock—tiny, hand-knitted, blue and green, clearly too old to belong to Otis.

Emma began to dread walking in there each morning. *It's leaving him gifts now.*

"I can't handle it," she said one night while they

lay in bed, both staring at the ceiling. "It's like some-one's leaving them for him. Not someone. It's gotta be the damn bear, right?"

Caleb turned his head toward her. "Don't say that. How could a stuffed bear possibly be responsible?"

"I mean it. Like offerings. Like the damn thing is watching, trying to buy his love."

"Emma, we're exhausted. We're not thinking straight."

But she was. She'd never felt more aware.

ONE NIGHT, as she rocked Otis back to sleep around 2 a.m., she noticed something new on the dresser—a baby spoon. Silver. Tarnished to a dull gray, with tiny teeth marks pressed into the handle. The name "Richard" was etched into the back in faint cursive. She didn't touch it.

All the clean blankets and onesies had been brushed to the floor. She told herself if she didn't acknowledge it, maybe it wouldn't be real.

THE LULLABY CAME BACK a few nights later. Twisted. *Backward?* Emma thought.

Emma had just finished feeding Otis. Caleb was brushing his teeth. She heard it as she was climbing into bed—a slow, warbling tune, like it was playing in reverse on warped cassette tape left in the sun. Twinkling and broken.

She froze. Her skin prickled.

It was coming from down the hall.

She stepped out of the bedroom just as Caleb opened the bathroom door.

"Do you hear that?" she asked.

He stopped mid-step. "What's up with that music?"

They followed it toward the nursery. The air in the hallway felt heavier with each step.

The moment Caleb's hand touched the knob, the music stopped.

Inside, everything looked the same. Otis's clothes folded neatly. The shelves untouched. No Cubby in sight.

But on the back of the door, above the knob, were three long scratches.

Fresh. And too high for their little Schnauzer to reach.

Thin grooves, deep enough to expose wood beneath paint. Clean. Deliberate.

Emma reached out and touched them before she

could stop herself. The edges were rough. Splintered.

She felt Caleb's hand wrap around hers, gently pulling her away. "That's it," he said, voice low. "We're done."

He didn't wait. He marched out of the room and up to the attic. He snatched Cubby from the chest and took him straight to the garage. Emma followed silently.

"Good thing it's trash day."

He stuffed the bear into a black trash bag, knotted it, double-bagged it, and tied it again.

He turned and didn't say a word as he walked it down to the end of the driveway and dropped it in the can. He put a brick on top for good measure. Emma watched from the doorway.

They didn't talk about it that night. They barely looked at each other. Otis woke twice. Neither of them got much sleep.

❌❌❌❌❌❌

IN THE MORNING, she looked out the front window and saw the trash bin was open on the curb. Empty. The garbage truck had come and gone.

Thank goodness.

Emma went to the nursery to get the baby ready for the day and stopped in the hallway. The smell hit her first—sour, damp, and clinging. A rank mix of rotting produce, curdled milk, and something meat-based gone foul. She breathed through her mouth and instantly regretted it. She could taste it now.

"Gross, we must have forgotten to empty the kitchen trash," she said to nobody.

She opened the door and froze.

Cubby was back.

In the rocking chair.

Same place. Same pose. Same bow. *Same smug stare, you little bastard.*

She rushed in to get Otis and went to find Caleb in the garage.

"The goddamn bear is *back,* and the hallway smells like old garbage." She grabbed his arm and led him to the nursery.

"I don't smell anything."

"It was so bad, I could *taste* it, I don't understand how it's gone."

"It doesn't matter., but this damn thing has to go for good."

He clenched his jaw, picked the bear up like it offended him to touch it, and carried it out of the house. He threw Cubby in another trash bag and drove away. She didn't ask where he was going. She stayed with Otis, pacing the living room.

WHEN HE CAME BACK, Caleb looked paler than before. His sleeves were damp.

"He's gone," he said, brushing past her. "I threw the bag in the river."

"You put a trash bag in the river?"

"Really, Em? That's the part you're concerned about?"

"Yes. I mean, no. I mean . . ." She bit her lip. "I don't want to see the damn thing ever again."

"Me either. Let's hope the little fucker can't swim."

"Did you just say *fucker* in front of our baby?"

"So did you."

Then they both laughed hysterically.

✘✘✘✘✘✘✘

THAT NIGHT, she dreamed of teeth.

Rows and rows of them—small, human, perfect—smiling in the dark. Not attached to faces. Just floating. Gleaming. Endless.

They chattered softly at first, like distant rain on a roof, then louder, until the sound turned to screaming. Not hers. Not his. Just screaming.

Cupcakes melted in the corners of her vision, their frosting bubbling along with the candle wax. Sprinkles burst like glass beneath her feet. The air smelled sweet—sickly sweet, scorched at the edges

—like burnt sugar and something darker underneath.

And then the flames came.

Slow at first. Elegant. Licking the wallpaper, curling it inward like old paper secrets. The screaming didn't stop. The teeth didn't stop. But everything else caught fire.

Even the shadows.

She tried to run, but the floor stuck to her soles —thick, tacky, like blood. Like syrup. Like something that wanted her to stay. The flames leaned toward her, hungry. Behind them, something small was watching.

Smiling.

❌❌❌❌❌❌

IN THE MORNING, the first thing she smelled was a mix of rot and silt in the air, thick and metallic.

No, no, no! She raced down to the nursery and flung the door open.

Sure enough, Cubby was back.

Emma didn't scream. She didn't faint.

She stared in disbelief.

He was in the crib this time. Bone-dry. His fur and bow were pristine.

His head tilted slightly forward like he'd been watching Otis sleep all night.

"Good morning!" Caleb called from the kitchen.

"Come here! You have to see this!"

Caleb sauntered in but stopped mid-step when he saw the looks on Emma's face. "You've got to be fucking kidding me!"

"We have to do something, Caleb."

There was a long pause.

"There's something I need to tell you about." She looked at the floor, then at him.

Caleb rubbed a hand over his face, slow and rough. "What are you talking about?"

"When we first moved in . . . I met someone. A woman named Margaret. She brought banana bread and gave me her number. Said she lived down the road."

"What banana bread? I don't remember having any banana bread."

"Gross! I threw it away. We don't eat food from . . . Never mind. That's not the important part."

"Why haven't you mentioned this?"

Emma hesitated. "It didn't seem important at the time. But she said something weird. About the house. That it had a long memory. That we should be careful about what we find in this house."

Caleb leaned against the counter. "You thought that wasn't worth telling me?"

"I didn't want to make it worse. I didn't know what she meant. And then everything started happening and I—" she trailed off.

"You think she knows something?"

Emma nodded. "I do."

They stood there for a while, letting the silence fill the space between them.

Then Caleb said, "Let's call her and see if she can help us."

Emma pulled out her phone, scrolled until she found the contact, and called. After a very brief exchange, she hung up and turned to Caleb.

"Let's get dressed, she wants us to meet her for breakfast."

1985

RICHARD DIDN'T MIND the laundromat.

It was quiet. Predictable. The hum of machines filled the space like white noise. No one looked too closely at you in a laundromat. Everyone was just trying to get through their chores.

That's why he came here most Thursdays after work. He had started coming a few months ago out of necessity after the washer finally broke for good and he couldn't afford the repair or the replacement. It gave him time to think. And to watch. He enjoyed it now. That's how he noticed her.

Tina. She was twenty-nine, newly divorced, and just starting over. Tina had a crooked smile and a habit of humming Madonna songs under her breath. She always arrived around 5:30. Folded her towels first, then her socks, then everything else. She brought a can of ginger ale and a fat paperback horror novel every week, always with cracked spines and bent corners. She sat in the same spot under the broken ceiling fan and read in silence. Tina had smiled at Richard once, weeks ago. It hadn't been flirtatious. Just polite. But it had lasted too long.

The bell over the door jingled and Tina walked in with her laundry bag slung over one shoulder. Richard was in a great mood today; it was his birthday. She didn't know that. No one did.

She smiled as she passed him. "Afternoon."

"Hi, Tina," he said.

"Hey, Richard. Funny running into you here."

Internally, he was rolling his eyes. But he laughed at her stupid joke. "Yep, time to make the donuts."

They loaded machines beside each other. Her detergent smelled like lavender. His didn't smell like anything. She laughed about how the fluorescent lights flickered above them.

"Feels like I'm doing laundry in a horror movie," she joked.

Richard laughed quietly. "Could be worse."

When the spin cycles started, they sat across

from each other. She read. He pretended to. But mostly, he watched. The way she tapped her heel in time with the dryer. The way she bent the spine of her book too far when she got to a scary part.

When her last machine buzzed, she stood and stretched. "Guess that's my cue."

"You heading out?"

"Yep. Fold and fly."

Richard hesitated, then said, "It's actually my birthday today."

Tina blinked, surprised. "Oh! Well, happy birthday, Richard."

"I brought cupcakes. Thought I'd share one with someone."

Her smile turned cautious. "Cupcakes?"

"Chocolate," he said. "Homemade. Still good."

She hesitated, then shrugged. "Okay. One. Then I've gotta head out."

"I'll help you load your car, and I'll give you one."

"That's so sweet, thank you."

Outside, the sky was turning dark as the last glimmers of daylight faded. Richard opened the passenger door of his car and pulled a plastic container from the seat. Inside: three cupcakes, perfectly frosted, with shiny little rainbow sprinkles.

"Looks like you already indulged."

"Nope. I always get just three of 'em." He offered one on a paper napkin. "Fresh."

She took it. Peeled back the wrapper. "Thanks. This is really nice of you."

He watched as she took a bite.

"Mm. Yeah, that's good."

"I'm glad," Richard said.

He sat beside her on the curb. The parking lot was nearly empty. They didn't talk for a while. A minute later, she blinked hard. Rubbed her temple.

"Huh. That's weird."

"What is?"

"Just got dizzy all of a sudden."

She tried to stand, but her legs buckled. Richard was already there, catching her gently. She didn't scream. She barely made a sound. She was unconscious before they reached his car.

🧸🧸🧸🧸🧸🧸

THE BARN SMELLED MUSTY, like dust, and oil, and fetid dirt. Richard had decided he couldn't do this in the house anymore, so he bought an old table and chairs from the thrift store to put out here for his parties. The table was already set, covered in a yellowed lace tablecloth. Two candles flickered in the center. The camera was loaded and waiting for him.

So was Cubby.

Richard had placed the bear there earlier in his seat of honor at the head of the table. The blue bow around his neck had been straightened up and his fur brushed for the special occasion. His glass eyes reflected the candlelight like mirrors. Cubby was already wearing his party hat.

He carried Tina in and laid her on the dirt floor of the barn. Her head lolled gently to the side. Still breathing. Still soft.

"Cubby," Richard whispered, "I brought you a gift. I wanted today to be special."

He stroked Tina's hair, pushed it back from her face. She looked like she was sleeping. He unwrapped the knife. It was nothing special, just something he'd picked up from Sears. But it wasn't about the blade—it was about the care of it. The intention. He worked slowly. Reverently.

The blood came quickly, warm and thick. It soaked into the soil in slow, dark spirals. He worked until the air felt still. Until the moment felt right.

Then he cleaned up as best he could. Wiped away the mess. Posed her arms and legs and smoothed her clothes. He brought Cubby from his chair and set him at her side.

"Look," he murmured, "She's right here. Just for you."

Then he lifted the Polaroid.

Framed the shot. Waited for the right moment.

Flash.

The burst of light filled the barn, and just as quickly, it was gone. Shadows returned. He waited for the photo to develop. When the image came through, he looked it over carefully.

A special moment. Frozen in time.

Richard leaned close and whispered, "Happy birthday, Cubby."

And in the flicker of candlelight, something shifted. Maybe the bear's head tilted. Or maybe it was just the shadows. But Richard smiled anyway. And Cubby was smiling too.

CHAPTER
NINE

Marta's Diner looked like it hadn't changed since the seventies.

One long stretch of windows, patched-up leather booths, and a jukebox that hadn't worked in years. A "Pies by the Slice" sign hung slightly crooked behind the counter, its letters sun-faded and curling. The waitress poured coffee like she was on autopilot, and nobody looked up when the bell over the door jingled.

Emma scanned the room and spotted Margaret in the corner booth, exactly where she said she'd be —window seat, cup of coffee, banana bread in Tupperware beside her like a peace offering. She looked older than Emma remembered. Or maybe just wearier. The kind of tired that settles into your joints.

Caleb hesitated beside her. Emma could feel the

tension in his hand where it gripped hers, but they both moved forward.

Margaret looked up and nodded. "Good morning," she said. "Sit down. You sounded spooked on the phone."

Emma slid into the booth. Caleb placed the car seat at her side and pulled a chair over from the next table.

"Thanks for meeting us," Emma said.

Margaret's expression didn't change. "I figured I'd be hearing from you, eventually."

She pushed the Tupperware toward them. "Banana bread. Still warm. I bake when I can't sleep."

Emma glanced at it. "Thank you. Not to rush, but you told me there was something wrong with the house."

"I did." Margaret folded her hands on the table. "And I stand by it."

Caleb leaned forward. "What do you know about it? About who lived there before?"

Margaret took a sip of coffee and exhaled like she was about to crack open something heavy.

"The Carver family lived there when I was little. I didn't know them well, but there was a boy. Richard. Quiet kid. Pale. Really strange child. We'd never see him walking around without that bear in his arms like it was part of him."

She paused, studying Emma's face.

Emma's stomach twisted. "We did find a bear. Its name is Cubby. It was written on the tag."

Margaret gave a single, slow nod. "Yeah. Same bear, I'd wager. That tracks."

Caleb blinked. "You knew him?"

"Not really," Margaret said. "But my brother did."

She turned her coffee mug in slow circles on the table.

"Tommy. That was my brother's name. He used to ride bikes with Richard. Said they'd play near the barn, mostly. That fall, they were inseparable. Until one day, Tommy didn't come home. That was the fall of 1967. He was eleven. I was nine."

Emma froze. "What happened?"

"We never found out," Margaret said. "One minute he was headed down the road to see his friend, the next minute . . . gone."

"Did they look for him?" Caleb asked.

"That's a stupid question. Of course we looked for him. Whole town turned out. Dogs. Flyers. News even did a segment. But nothing. No body, no bike, no sign. My mom stopped saying his name after the first month. Told me not to ask questions." Her eyes hardened. "But I remember what I heard."

Emma leaned in. "What?"

"Sheriff questioned the Carver boy. He said he hadn't seen Tommy that day. But . . ." Margaret's voice faltered. "Tommy had told me where he was going. Said he got invited to a birthday party."

Caleb sat back. "A party?"

Margaret nodded. "He said it was Richard's twelfth birthday, and he was going after school for a party. October third, 1967. I'll never forget that day."

Emma's breath hitched. "That's our baby's birthday."

The silence that followed was brittle.

Emma looked down at the table, suddenly nauseated.

Margaret broke the silence. "I don't know what's happening in there now. But I know how it started. That boy, Richard—he wasn't right. Not even then. And the bear? It was always with him. Damn thing looked brand new no matter how long he had it. Clean. Like it didn't belong in this world."

She looked at Emma, then Caleb. "If you're still in that house, you need to be very careful."

Emma swallowed hard. "We tried to get rid of it. We did everything."

Margaret's eyes flicked between them, sad and tired. "You can't throw away something like that. Not if it's already chosen you."

"How do you know it's the bear doing all of this and not someone else?" Caleb demanded. "Maybe it's Richard, maybe he's been living in the attic?"

Emma looked horrified.

"You think you're the first family to move in

there? Last family told me about finding a bear in the attic and how they gave it to their boy. They lasted about three months in that place, and they didn't even say goodbye when they left. Just packed up and I never saw them again."

Margaret sighed, slow and deliberate. "You're not the first, and you won't be the last. But if you're smart, you won't stay."

Emma leaned back, her hand resting protectively on Otis beside her.

"Now, tell me everything," Margaret said.

And they did. About finding the bear. The way it would appear in a new location. The way it never got dirty. The trinkets and gifts. The notebook. Emma's dreams. The music. The scratches in the door.

Caleb narrowed his eyes. "So. You said it's chosen us. What does that mean? What does it want?"

Margaret didn't answer right away. She looked past them, out the window, as if watching something that hadn't arrived yet.

Then she said, quiet and certain, "It never wanted the house."

Emma stared at her.

"It wanted the child."

The words settled between them like a drop of ink in water—small but spreading.

Caleb's jaw tightened. Emma felt the blood

drain from her face. Her hand instinctively moved to her chest, like shielding her heart might somehow protect her son.

"I—I don't understand," Emma whispered.

Margaret's gaze came back to her. "It's not about the house, I think. It's about who it attaches to. That bear, it's not just haunted, if that's what you're thinking. It's tied to something. Maybe that boy, Richard. Maybe what he did. But probably before that. I have a feeling that bear is ancient. Or at least what lives in it is. But the longer you stay, the closer it gets."

"To what? What did he do?" Caleb asked.

"Nothing is official, you see. But a bunch of people suspected he had something to do with folks disappearing around here. Almost every October, somebody went missing. Go look it up for yourself. Nobody ever proved it though. And then one day Richard disappeared. Vanished. *Poof.* At first, they thought he may have died in the barn fire at his house, your house. But one of the neighbors called it in pretty quick, so when they came to put it out, it was only partly burned down, and nobody was in it."

Emma swallowed. "So, what are we supposed to do? Leave the house?"

Margaret shook her head. "I don't know. I've never seen anyone stop it."

"Did you just ask us here to get your gossip fix?

You asked us to tell you everything, and we did. Now it's your turn. You're not helping," Caleb snapped.

Margaret's expression hardened. "I'm not here to help. I'm here because she asked me for what I know. And I told you what I know." She nodded toward Emma. "She called me and said something was wrong. And I told you, didn't I? I told you back then to be careful with what you find up there."

Emma nodded faintly. "You did."

Margaret leaned forward, elbows on the table. "You think the scratches are the worst of it? The missing hours? The dreams? That's just noise. That's the warm-up. It's coming for him." She glanced at Otis.

Caleb's face was pale now. "But . . . he's just a baby."

"I know," Margaret said. "That's the point."

Nobody spoke.

A server passed behind them, dropping off fresh coffee at another table. The clink of porcelain, the scratch of chairs, the hum of a tired jukebox trying to spin to life and failing.

Margaret didn't blink. "I can't tell you what to do next. But I can tell you this—every minute you wait, it gets more comfortable."

Emma looked at the banana bread.

"Do you want it?" Margaret asked.

Emma shook her head.

"I didn't think so." Margaret slid the Tupperware back toward herself and stood.

"If you stay, watch that baby like a hawk." She pointed at Otis. "Don't leave him alone in that room. Don't let the bear near him." She paused, looking for the right words. "And don't ever assume it's done because it's quiet."

She tucked the bread under her arm and turned to leave.

"Margaret," Emma said, voice catching in her throat. "Thank you."

Margaret didn't smile. She only said, "Be fast." And pushed open the door.

The bell over it jingled once. Then silence.

Caleb stared down at the table.

Emma reached for his hand, but his fingers were still clenched into a fist.

They sat like that for another minute, neither of them speaking. The waitress dropped the check without asking. Someone laughed at the counter, too loud for the room.

Emma slid out of the booth first.

Outside, the sun was too bright. The wind too still.

They walked to the car in silence. Caleb unlocked it, but neither of them got in right away. Emma leaned against the passenger door, arms crossed.

"She's right, you know," she said quietly.

Caleb didn't look at her. "About what?"

"All of it."

He ran a hand through his hair and stared back toward the diner like he might see Margaret again.

When he finally turned, his voice was flat. "Then we stop pretending it's normal."

I never thought this was normal! Emma thought, but this was not the time to start an argument, so she nodded instead.

They got into the car. Otis stirred in his car seat, letting out a soft, sleepy sound that broke the silence as Emma popped it back into the base. Emma laid a gentle hand on his chest to soothe him.

The engine started. And they drove home, not speaking, both of them bracing for what might be waiting inside.

1987

THE BOWLING ALLEY buzzed with noise and neon, cheap beer, and the smell of spray disinfectant and stale cheese fries. The speakers were loud and distorted—someone had put on a Blondie cassette and the treble was way too high. It didn't matter. Richard wasn't here for the music.

He stepped inside wearing a black windbreaker and a cheap paper party hat. Blue with yellow stars. He walked up to the counter.

"Shoes," he said.

The kid behind the counter barely looked up from his *MAD* magazine. "Size?"

"Ten and a half."

A pair of grimy rentals hit the counter. Richard took them and sat on the nearest bench to change out of his boots. He slid the old shoes on carefully. The leather was cracked, and the left sole was coming loose, but they'd do.

Once laced, he moved to the rack of bowling balls. They were garish—striped, swirled, marbled in every color like melted candy. He ignored them all except one. Matte black, no visible brand name, heavier than most. He lifted it gently and carried it to lane 15. Near the wall. Near the dark.

Next to him, lane 14 buzzed with energy and the confident laughter of grown women. Late twenties, maybe thirty. All of them drinking cheap beer out of clear plastic cups, smoking menthols, eating limp pizza from paper plates.

The one in the middle was the loudest. The brightest. Everything about her said: *center of attention*. He heard the other women call her Carla.

She had long dark hair, teased high, and neon pink nails that flashed under the blacklights every time she raised her hands to talk. Her voice carried effortlessly—low, confident, the kind of voice that had told men off before and would again. She wasn't the best bowler of the group, but she was the one everyone watched anyway. Richard sat still and watched her, his hand resting lightly on the ball. She saw him eventually. Alone. Paper hat. Just sitting. Not bowling. Not drinking. Not eating. Watching.

She paused mid-laugh and leaned toward her friend. "Creep alert," she exclaimed and pointed at him.

Her friend followed her gaze. Shrugged. "Ignore him. Probably waiting for a league game."

Carla took another drink. But she glanced back one more time. Longer. Good. Richard waited.

Eventually, one woman was picked up by her boyfriend. Another said her sitter had a time limit. Slowly, the group thinned. Coats were slung over arms. Lipstick was reapplied in the mirror beside the restroom sign. Carla stayed behind. She leaned on the lane's scoring table, sipping the last of her beer and tapping her nail absently on the side of the cup.

Richard stood.

He walked to the ball return and picked up black ball. Let his fingers settle into the holes, weight pressing into his palm like a slow heartbeat. Then he stepped to the lane and watched her.

She noticed right away.

"Okay, great," she said aloud, half to herself. "That guy's still here."

No one answered. The alley was emptying. The music faded as someone turned the volume down. One of the staff started sweeping popcorn into a plastic dustpan.

Richard rolled the ball.

CRACK.

A perfect strike. The pins exploded and vanished behind the curtain.

He turned.

"Happy birthday," he said softly.

Carla blinked. "Uh . . . thanks? But it's not my birthday."

"It's mine," he said.

Her voice caught, then rose into a nervous laugh. "Well, happy birthday, I guess."

She slung her purse over one shoulder and stepped away from the lane. "My ride's late," she said aloud. "They should be here any second."

"No one's coming, Carla."

She froze. Her gaze darted toward the front doors. No headlights outside. No one was visible inside, most of the staff had either gone home or were out back in the break room. She started walking—fast—but not running. Richard moved faster.

He caught her near the vending machine, hand gripping her shoulder hard enough to twist her off-balance. She stumbled. Her purse hit the ground with a heavy *thud*, lipstick and change spilling out.

"What the hell—" she started.

He shoved her. Her back hit the wall with a hollow whomp and she fell down.

She scrambled upright. Limping. Her ankle had turned. "Help!" she shouted, but it barely rose above the sound of someone vacuuming the arcade carpet.

Richard lifted the ball. Held it like something holy.

"People never celebrate the day right," he said.

Her eyes were wide. "You're outta your goddamn mind—"

"Make a wish."

He brought the ball down.

CRACK.

The sound was wet and final.

The second hit came fast.

The third . . . *Well, that one was overkill.*

He stood still for a moment, listening. They were still vacuuming. No screams. No running. He stepped around the body. Picked up the ball. Wiped it off and carried it back to the return rack like nothing had happened. He unlaced the rental shoes slowly, placed them back on the counter, then stepped into his boots. He picked Carla up and slipped out the back door.

Outside, the parking lot buzzed with a faulty neon sign. BOWL-O-RAMA blinked and stuttered. He opened the back door and laid Carla in the back-seat. When he got around to the front of his car,

Cubby was waiting in the passenger seat. Upright. Bow tied. Party hat on. His obsidian eyes reflected the neon lights in two tiny flashes. Richard shut the door behind him, started the engine, and looked over at the bear. Then smiled.

"Happy birthday," he whispered. "Let's get out of here."

CHAPTER
TEN

They didn't say much on the drive home. Otis slept the whole way, his soft breathing the only sound in the car.

Caleb gripped the steering wheel like it might try to steer itself. Emma stared out the window, arms folded tight across her chest.

The house looked the same when they pulled up. That was part of the problem.

It was always the same.

The door creaked the same. The wind nudged the shutters the same. Cubby was nowhere in sight, but Emma didn't trust that for a second. She carried Otis straight to the living room and kept him in her lap while Caleb powered up his laptop and slid it onto the kitchen table.

"Let's see this for ourselves. I'll try the newspaper archives," he said. "There's got to be something online."

Emma nodded. "Let's start with October 1967 articles."

He did.

The first few pages were slow going—anniversary stories, harvest festivals, school calendars. Then, about halfway down the third page of results, Caleb's hand froze on the trackpad.

"Here," he said.

Emma stood and moved behind him. The headline was black and white, grainy with age:

LOCAL BOY, 11, DISAPPEARS ON WAY TO BIRTHDAY PARTY

October 5, 1967, Tommy James, age 11, vanished Tuesday afternoon on his way to a friend's house.

Emma leaned in. "That's Margaret's brother."

Caleb clicked through. "The article says he was last seen riding his bike down Miller Road. That's—"

"Two roads over from us," Emma finished.

They kept searching.

Next page:

LOCAL TEEN MISSING AFTER WEEKEND OUTING

October 6, 1970, Sean Davis, 15, was reported missing Saturday evening after failing to return home.

Then another:

CORNER STORE EMPLOYEE REPORTED MISSING

October 5, 1973, Leah Chamberlain, 17, was last seen leaving work late Wednesday evening. Family says she mentioned going to a friend's party.

Another year. Another October.
Emma glanced at Otis, still asleep on her chest.
Caleb's voice was tight. "That's three."
He scrolled again.

GROCERY CLERK FAILS TO RETURN HOME AFTER SHIFT

October 4, 1977, Marlene Simmons, 22, disappeared from the Market Mart parking lot. Coworkers report no suspicious behavior prior.

"This is insane. Look." He pointed at the screen.

WOMAN MISSING AFTER WEEKLY LAUNDRY RUN

October 4, 1985, Tina Holbrook, 29, last seen at Eastwood Laundromat. Vehicle found abandoned.

The articles piled up—always vague, always around the same date. None of the missing persons were ever found and the authorities never seemed to have any leads.

So many disappearances. All in or near their town. All clustered around Richard's birthday.

Emma sat down slowly beside Caleb. "That can't be a coincidence."

He didn't argue.

They sat in silence for a long moment, the only sound the soft rhythmic breath of Otis sleeping in her arms.

She stared at the laptop screen. One of the photos showed a black-and-white picture of Leah Chamberlain, smiling from behind a cash register.

"She was just a kid," Emma whispered.

Finally, Caleb said, "We need to go deeper. Background checks, family names, property records. If this all ties back to Richard . . ."

Emma shook her head. "It's not just him. Margaret said the bear has always looked new. Like it didn't belong in this world."

"I think he was . . . I don't know." Caleb fidgeted. "Or maybe—" he stopped himself.

Emma looked at him. "Maybe what?"

"Maybe the bear was, I don't know, this sounds crazy. But maybe the bear was helping him."

Her stomach twisted, and her thoughts tangled right along with it.

"Let me put him down for a nap, and then I want to look at one more thing."

She took Otis to the nursery, checked every-where for Cubby, and placed him in the crib when she didn't see the bear.

"Sweet dreams," she said, kissing him to the forehead.

On her way back, she stopped in the kitchen to retrieve the notebook they had left on the counter—the one from the attic. The one that didn't stop calling to her, even when it was closed.

She took it to the living room, turned to the middle, and read aloud:

"She said I had to stop bringing him to the table. But Cubby's always hungry."

Caleb glanced over her shoulder.

Emma flipped to the next page. Another scrawl:

"Don't like the red crayon. He makes me use it."

Her fingers trembled slightly.

"He wasn't just talking to the bear," she said softly. "He was taking orders."

Caleb didn't respond. He just looked at the page —at the uneven handwriting, the frantic spacing, the heavy pressure of the lines.

Emma turned one more page.

At the bottom, in smaller, tighter letters:

"He remembers everything."

She stared at the words, her mouth dry.

Caleb leaned closer. "Who does?"

Emma closed the notebook gently. "I don't think he meant himself."

A soft click echoed through the house. Emma turned sharply toward the nursery. They went down the hall and pushed the door open.

Otis was asleep in in his crib.

No Cubby.

She turned toward Caleb. "He's not in the nursery."

Caleb was already moving away.

They searched the house. The porch. The car.

Nothing.

Then Emma opened the laundry room.

There he was.

Sitting on the dryer.

Bow straight. Tag sticking out.

Exactly as clean as the day they found him.

Emma backed out slowly and closed the door.

"We need a new plan," she said.

Caleb didn't argue.

He glanced at the closed laundry room door, then back at her. "One last try."

Emma raised an eyebrow. "You have something in mind?"

He nodded slowly. "Not the trash, not the attic, and not a box in the shed. I mean gone. We drive. Far."

She didn't ask what he meant. She was on board with any way to make it stop.

"Okay," she said. "We'll go when he wakes up."

�✠✠✠✠✠

THEY DIDN'T SPEAK MUCH while getting ready. Emma tucked Otis into his car seat. Caleb brought the fireproof gloves he used for the grill and a gas can he kept in the garage. It all felt like overkill. It also felt like the bare minimum.

Cubby was exactly where they'd left him— sitting on the dryer, like someone had adjusted him for display. Caleb didn't flinch. He grabbed the bear by the middle and carried him outside without a word. Emma didn't follow right away. She stood in the doorway for a few seconds, watching that space where Cubby had been, already imagining the next time he'd be there again.

But she followed. She always would. She got the baby situated in his car seat while Caleb loaded supplies, and the bear, into the trunk.

They drove two hours out of town. No music. Otis slept most of the way, and when he didn't, he gurgled softly to himself in the back seat, unaware of the thing that had wrapped its shadow around his family was mere inches away.

The spot Caleb picked was an old county park off Route 38, a place they'd passed before but never visited. Empty that day. Just picnic tables, a broken

swing set, and a rusting metal barrel meant for charcoal fires and trash.

Perfect.

Emma stood back and held Otis on her hip while
Caleb placed the bear inside the barrel. He doused it
in gasoline, then stepped back.

"You ready?" he asked.

Emma nodded.

Caleb struck a match, let it burn for a few
seconds, then tossed it in.

The fire whooshed to life—quick, bright, star-
tling. Flames leapt, clawed, and danced. The smell
was awful. Synthetic fur, stuffing, something sharp
and chemical beneath the gasoline. Emma watched
the velvet bow curl and blacken. The seams gave
way, and the whole thing folded in on itself, a
blackened mass collapsing under its own weight.

The glass eyes didn't melt. They dropped into
the ash like smooth stones, glossy and unburned,
catching the firelight even after the flames began
to die.

They stayed until it was ash.

Caleb used a stick to stir the remains. Nothing
recognizable remained—just char, dust, and the
twin glint of those eyes staring up from the center.

Emma didn't speak, just stood with Otis
bundled tight against her, his tiny head pressed to
her shoulder. Her eyes stung, but she didn't cry.

When it was done, Caleb poured water from a

plastic bottle over the embers and watched the hiss of steam rise. The barrel smoked. The wind carried it away.

Back in the car, Caleb looked at her. "That should be the end of it."

She didn't answer.

In the rearview mirror, the fire barrel shrank behind them, just a rusted shape disappearing into the trees.

But she could still picture those glass eyes—buried in ash—plotting.

1990

RICHARD DIDN'T BELIEVE in fate, but he believed in patterns. In cycles. He thought he heard Billy Donaldson in the break room two months ago, laughing with another mid-level nobody about someone's shoes. That laugh, nasally, smug, the same it had been in elementary school, made something twist in Richard's chest. Then he saw the nose. Just a little crooked. Barely noticeable unless you were the one who broke it.

They were seven. Billy had cornered him at recess, tried to yank Cubby away from him, and shoved him face-first into the gravel. Called him "Baby Richie." Said he smelled like ketchup and dirty underwear.

Richard hit him with a rock.

One clean shot.

He remembered the blood and the teacher screaming. The school called it "unprovoked."

Billy forgot.

But Richard never did.

Now, almost thirty years later, they were both working in the same building. Richard worked for a mail-order catalog doing data entry. Billy hadn't changed much. But now he wore ugly, loud ties and sold insurance. He still laughed with his whole face. Still carried himself like a boy who never got punished long enough to learn a lesson.

Richard watched. Waited. Billy always stayed late on Thursdays. Richard's birthday fell on Thursday this year.

Perfect.

Richard carried a white box and his backpack down the hallway to the shared break room which was also the copier room around 7 pm. The office suites were quiet. The overhead light was flickering, as always.

Billy was hunched over the Xerox machine, swearing at it.

"Goddamn stupid thing, always out of fucking toner," he muttered.

"Hey," Richard said.

Billy looked up, toner smudged on his crooked little nose. "Oh, hey, man. If you need the copier, you're shit outta luck. You work for the catalog, right?"

Richard nodded. "Yeah. Just thought I'd share something."

He placed the white box on the table beside the copier.

Billy gave a half-smile, unsure. "What's the occasion?"

"It's my birthday."

"No kidding? Well, happy birthday. Are you getting out of here soon?"

"Soon."

Billy walked over to the table and opened the box. "Nice cupcakes. Looks homemade."

"I make three every year."

"Why only three? That's a pretty weird tradition."

Richard studied him. The way he rubbed the bridge of his nose, like he always had.

He watched Billy look down at the cupcakes, then back up, head tilting slightly.

"You look familiar," Billy said, narrowing his eyes. "But not from the office. I can't quite place it."

Richard's lips barely moved. "Yes."

Billy laughed. "Where?"

"You don't remember me."

That made Billy pause. Just for a second.

Then he smiled again. "Nah, man, I'm terrible with names. Sorry."

Richard's hand was already in his coat pocket.

Billy didn't notice the wire until it looped around his throat.

The struggle was clumsy—loud. Billy shoved backward, knocking into the copier. Toner spilled across the floor. He gasped, fingers clawing at the garrote. The muscles in Richard's arms ached, but he didn't let go. He couldn't let go.

This wasn't *just* a ritual.

This was everything, his purpose, an act of love for his only friend, not only remembered, but carved into muscle and breath. Taking a life meant nothing. Honoring one was all that mattered.

Billy bucked once more. Then stilled.

Richard lowered him to the floor, careful not to drop him in the toner spill. He dragged him over to a chair and seated the body upright, adjusting the posture. He wiped blood from the wire with the corner of Billy's tie.

He removed the cupcakes from the box, placed a candle in each, and lit them. Next, he removed Cubby from his backpack and posed him in Billy's lap, arranging the cupcakes in front of them on the table. Then he pulled out the party hats and placed one on everyone's head. *It wouldn't be much of a party without hats, would it?*

"Happy Birthday to us, Cubby." He removed his Polaroid camera and took the photo. "Bet you remember now, asshole," he whispered to Billy. Then he blew the candles out.

Richard cleaned up the blood, put everything back where it went, and packed all of his things into his backpack. *Toner is someone else's problem tomorrow.* He loaded Billy in the back of his car and buckled Cubby into the passenger seat.

"This one gets an extra special spot in the barn," he said to Cubby. Richard had already dug the hole in the dirt floor of the barn. And in the hole, he had emptied twenty-eight bottles of ketchup, one for every birthday since the incident in second grade, and added a few pairs of his ratty, old, threadbare underwear.

CHAPTER
ELEVEN

Nearly four weeks had passed without incident.

Emma stopped flinching at shadows. Caleb no longer checked the attic door before bed. The notebook stayed closed, tucked inside a drawer beneath a stack of insurance papers and old coupons. No new scratches. No strange gifts. No lullabies.

The nursery became a nursery. Otis slept longer stretches. The rocking chair stayed still. Cubby was gone, really gone. Emma sometimes allowed herself the luxury of forgetting. She folded onesies without expecting them to be moved. She opened the baby monitor app without dread. She sang to Otis while changing his diaper, and he gurgled in response.

They even cleaned out the attic.

It had been Emma's idea. A final purge of whatever still lingered—old furniture, boxes with stained labels, the crumbling remains of that little bed in the hidden room. They cleared it all. Caleb borrowed a friend's truck and hauled everything to the dump in one exhausting weekend.

And that was when they found the shoebox.

Tucked behind a beam, wedged into a hollow space in the wall. Covered in dust. Wrapped with duct tape, layers upon layers of it. Caleb had paused when he pulled it free. "You want me to open it?"

Emma had nodded, though her stomach already knew the answer.

Inside were bones.

Small. Fragile. Arranged on a bit of fabric, as if someone had once tried to tuck them in. The remains of a small animal, long since turned to dust and splinters. A rusted bell collar lay in the corner, the metal eaten through in spots. One glassy eye sat loose among the remains, like it had been pulled from a toy. Or something else. And a small note, written in crayon, that read *STUPID FERRET*.

Caleb threw the box out without saying much. Emma didn't want any details.

They told themselves the attic was empty now. Cleansed. The past reduced to trash bags and disposal runs.

Caleb returned to work. Emma made muffins and gave some to Margaret. They had become friends of sorts—Margaret didn't stop by often, but when she did, she always brought something: fresh herbs, homemade soap, a small jar of pickled onions. She never stayed long, and she never asked questions.

Daisy curled up in the sun again. She sniffed Otis's head and wagged her tail when Emma passed by. The tension that had once gripped the house seemed to dissolve, leaving behind something that almost resembled peace.

That evening, Emma and Caleb sat on the couch, a movie flickering on mute while Otis slept in his crib down the hall. A soft baby monitor hiss came from Emma's phone. The rocking chair on screen was still. The mobile above the crib was still.

"Hard to believe," Caleb said, arm draped across the back of the couch.

Emma nodded. "I almost feel guilty for relaxing."

"Don't," he said. "You've earned it."

They didn't talk about the bear. They didn't have to.

Later, they brushed their teeth in silence, trading sleepy smiles and shared yawns. They were finally comfortable letting Otis sleep in his room. Emma peeked in on him before bed, then closed the nursery door until it clicked shut.

Everything had become so normal.

But routine has a way of seducing you.

Lulling you into complacency.

✗✗✗✗✗✗

JUST BEFORE 2 A.M., Emma was jolted from sleep.

The sound was loud and warped. She sat upright to make sure she wasn't dreaming.

The lullaby.

That same crooked tune—music box slow, dragging like a warped cassette, playing from somewhere in the house.

No. *Everywhere* in the house.

"Caleb!!"

"You hear it too?"

They both scrambled from bed. Emma grabbed the monitor.

The screen flickered briefly, then stabilized.

Otis. He was in the crib, crying. His little fists clenched, face red and twisted.

Nothing else moved.

Emma's voice shook. "He's crying! Holy shit, this music, how!?"

They jumped up to race to Otis. Emma grabbed her phone from the nightstand in case they needed to call someone.

Caleb was already halfway down the hall when the lights snapped off.

Darkness swallowed them.

The music didn't stop.

Emma flicked the flashlight function on and

followed him, her pulse thudding in her ears. As they reached the bottom of the stairs and turned toward the nursery—

There he was.

Cubby.

Perfect. Unburned. Sitting upright just outside the nursery door, his blue velvet bow tied neatly around his neck.

The same bear they had watched burn to ash.

Emma stopped cold. "No!!"

Caleb saw it too. "You've got to be kidding me."

Otis screamed from inside the nursery.

Emma rushed forward and grabbed the doorknob—it didn't turn. "It's locked!"

Caleb threw himself at the door. "Move! I'll break it open!"

The bear sat still and watched.

Emma looked down—and Cubby blinked at her.

She kicked it with everything she had.

Cubby flew down the hall, hit the wall, and bounced once before sliding toward the kitchen.

The music warbled on. A greenish light oozed through the gap at the bottom of the door, like swamp water, thick and sickly, with a hue somewhere between rotting lettuce and bile. It made the shadows look diseased and gave the air a faint shimmer like heat rising off garbage.

She could barely hear herself think over the crying—so raw and so close—and the lullaby's stuttered loop. Every hair on her arms stood on end. The house no longer felt like theirs.

Caleb returned a minute later with a tire iron from the garage. He was breathing hard, barefoot, his shoulders tense and ready.

Emma stepped aside. "Do it!"

He bashed the handle into the doorknob—once, twice—until the wood splintered and the latch gave.

They rushed inside.

The music stopped. No light.

The crib was empty.

No Otis.

Emma's scream caught in her throat. "No, no, he was just here!"

She tore back the blankets, checked the floor, and turned in circles. "Otis!"

Caleb yanked open the closet. Nothing. He dropped to his knees and looked under the crib, frantic. "He's not here! He's not—"

Then they heard it.

Crying.

Muffled. Higher up. The lullaby began again, louder this time.

They locked eyes.

"The attic," Emma yelled.

And then they ran.

Caleb reached the hallway first, his footsteps thunderous against the hardwood floor. Emma followed close behind, her chest tight, heart punching inside her ribs. The house suddenly felt taller than it was, filled with corners she didn't remember, walls that seemed to lean inward with each step.

They turned the corner—

And the attic door was open.

Just a crack. Not wide, but enough to know it hadn't been that way before. Through the narrow gap, a pale light wavered—puny and unclean—like the last flicker of a dying fire, or something trying to mimic warmth but getting it just slightly, disturbingly wrong.

Caleb reached for the handle.

The crying continued above them—thin and gasping, like Otis was running out of steam. Emma shoved past him and pushed the attic door open all the way.

The narrow stairs stretched upward into shadow.

No wind. No sound other than the baby's cries. And that terrible, sweet lullaby reverberating as if the walls themselves were humming along.

"I'm going," Emma said, already on the first step.

"I'm right behind you," Caleb whispered.

The stairs creaked as they climbed, old wood shifting beneath hurried feet. The temperature dropped as they rose—so sharply that Emma gasped by the time she reached the top.

Emma stepped out into the attic space, Caleb only a breath behind her.

She turned slowly.

The cedar chest was open again.

And in the very back, where the hidden room door had once been sealed—

Now it gaped wide, with the same pulsing, green light emanating from inside.

Emma's breath caught. The small room inside had changed.

The child-sized bed still sat crooked against the far wall. The melted toys remained, the wallpaper still peeling like dead skin, and on the blistered yellow table, sat three cupcakes with burning birthday candles.

And now, there was a crib.

Their crib.

Moved. Placed here.

"What the actual . . ." Caleb said.

Otis lay inside it.

His cheeks were flushed with effort; tiny hands balled at his chest. He wailed—loud and hoarse and angry.

Emma ran forward.

But she stopped short.

There, beside the crib, sat the rocking chair.

And in it—

Cubby.

Blue velvet bow tied just right.

His glass eyes reflected the amber glow.
The bear didn't move.
But the chair did.
Rocking.
Slowly.
Back and forth.
Back and forth.

1994

THE COFFEE POT was down to sludge. Richard could smell it before he pushed the door open—burnt, bitter, sharp. He didn't mind. That kind of smell didn't bother him anymore.

Marta's Diner sat at the edge of town near Route 38, open all night but half-asleep by two in the morning. The "OPEN" sign buzzed like an angry insect against the glass. Inside, the booths were empty. A jukebox in the corner cycled through old country songs like it was too tired to care. Conway Twitty warbled beneath the buzz of fluorescent lights.

Richard stepped inside. The bell above the door gave a half-hearted jingle.

The waitress at the counter didn't look up right

away. She was scrubbing something that didn't want to come off of the Formica countertop.

He waited, still in the doorway, until she finally turned. She looked tired, late-thirties, the kind of tired that lived in her shoulders, not just her eyes. A cigarette dangled from her fingers. Her name tag said Janine.

"Coffee, please," he said.

His voice was soft. Flat. He couldn't remember the last time he'd meant the words.

She poured him a cup without asking if he wanted decaf. "Cream?"

He shook his head.

He took the mug and walked to the last booth in the far corner. The vinyl seat let out a slow sigh as he slid into it. He didn't sip the coffee. Didn't even smell it.

Outside, in the near-dark parking lot, his car sat crooked, taking up two parking spots. He hadn't bothered to park properly. No one would tow him. Not at this hour.

He put a brown paper grocery bag in the seat of the booth and set his paperback down on the table. It was a fat novel with a cracked spine and hollowed-out center. It had belonged to Tina, and it made a great place to hide things. *Like drugs,* Richard mused. *Nobody would ever check a shitty old book.*

He watched the reflection of the open sign dance in the window for a long time. Didn't look at the

135

coffee. The cupcakes were still in the bag. Vanilla, with chocolate frosting. A package of blue birthday candles. He'd bought these that very afternoon at the grocery store. He didn't have the energy to make his own this year. He was tired. Not sleepy—tired. The kind that lived in your soul. The kind that came after years of promises that didn't quite come to fruition.

Another birthday.

He promised me we'd stop when I became a grown-up. And here I am, thirty-nine goddamn years old, still at it. Every year it's the same thing. But Cubby comes up with a new rule every time I bring it up. "We can stop when," he always tells me.

Cubby's last promise was they could stop when Richard's bitch of a mother was dead. After all, Cubby *did* protect him from her. He always had, in his own way. His mom knew something was up. She hated his friendship with Cubby, and she was afraid of Richard because of it. She knew something was *off* about him.

But she needs me. She can't hardly do anything for herself these days. And if I gift her to Cubby, the social security checks stop, and then where would we go? They always find a bullshit reason to can me from every job I get and I can't afford—

He startled with surprise when Janine came around to refill his coffee.

Shit. I didn't get a chance to fix up the cupcakes. Good thing I always have a backup plan.

"Need a top-up?" she asked.

Richard looked up. His eyes were pale and steady. "I brought you something," he said.

She froze, halfway between polite detachment and suspicion. "What?"

He pushed the brown paper bag toward her.

"Don't worry," he said. "It's just cupcakes." He though for second then added, "From the store."

She opened it cautiously, peeled the top back. Chocolate frosting. Birthday candles.

She snorted. "Why on earth would you bring me cupcakes?"

"It's mine," he said, in a tone that was more ominous than celebratory.

She raised an eyebrow.

"My birthday. Today."

"Well, happy birthday, stranger, But I ain't eating food from a bag handed to me by a guy who talks to himself."

Richard didn't smile. "I just didn't want to spend it alone."

Janine hesitated, maybe out of pity. Maybe out of something else. But she didn't walk away fast enough.

He moved to grab her before she could blink.

The coffee pot shattered against the floor. Her arms flailed as she fell, hitting the edge of the booth's table hard. She gasped, the wind knocked out of her.

Richard didn't shout. Didn't grunt. Just moved with that same flat stillness he carried everywhere. Efficient. Inevitable.

He reached into his jacket pocket and retrieved the length of piano wire, wound tight around two wooden pegs. The very same one he'd used on Billy Donaldson.

He pulled it free.

Janine tried to scream. He looped it around her throat before the sound left her mouth. She clawed at him. Kicked. Knocked the ceramic mug across the table—it exploded into shards, one catching her in the cheek, another slicing her palm.

He didn't flinch. He pulled the wire tight. Firm. Familiar. Her resistance faded quickly. Her hands fell. He kept the wire in place a moment longer than necessary. Just to be sure. Then let her slip. The jukebox hummed into the next song. A woman, singing something about falling to pieces.

Richard sat back. Stared at her face. Blood at the corner of her mouth. Apron stained. He picked her up and propped her in the booth, careful not to spill her completely onto the seat. Smoothed her hair, reset the collar of her uniform.

He wasn't angry. Just empty. Too many birthdays. Too many cupcakes and meaningless wishes. He sat down next to her and finished his coffee. He leaned forward until his lips were just above her ear.

"Thank you," he whispered, voice hoarse. "For celebrating with me." Then he left a dollar on the table, gathered his things, picked up Janine and headed back to the car.

Outside, the wind had picked up. He flopped Janine into the trunk, then opened his door and climbed in, the seat cold under him. Cubby waited patiently in the passenger seat for his gift.

Richard stared at the wheel. He didn't start the car. He sat in the silence and wondered—not for the first time—if this would be the last one. He thought about the first time he brought Cubby someone. The nervous excitement. The certainty. The promise. That feeling was gone now. Tonight had been quiet. Mechanical. Like cleaning out a closet. He was growing tired of everything.

"Well, happy birthday," he said again, this time to no one in particular. "Let's get her home and have our cupcakes. And before you ask, yes, we'll get a party photo before we put her with the others."

Cubby blinked once but didn't reply.

Richard started the car.

TWELVE

They stood frozen just inside the attic room, Otis's cries splitting the stale air. Caleb was right beside her, breath loud in the hush, the tire iron still clutched in one hand. They hadn't spoken since they saw the crib—*their* crib—sitting neatly against the wall like it had always belonged there.

Emma stepped forward.

"Don't," Caleb said quickly. "Wait—think."

"He's crying," she said through gritted teeth. "He's right there. We can't just—"

Emma hesitated for half a breath.

Otis's cries wavered—sharp, panicked, real. But the longer she looked at him, the more wrong it felt. He was swaddled exactly the way she'd left him hours ago. Too exactly. His face was flushed, his lips trembling, but something about the stillness around him made her blood run cold. Her legs wanted to run, but her body moved like it was underwater. She told herself to breathe. Told herself the baby was real.

Otis wailed again, high and full of rage.

Cubby's head tilted.

Just slightly.

It was enough.

Emma lunged for the crib.

The bear didn't move—but something in the room did. A shift in the air. A hum beneath the floorboards. A breeze whipped through the room, extinguishing the birthday candles.

Emma scooped Otis into her arms, backing away. Caleb reached for her but stopped when the rocking chair began to creak—slow, steady, building speed without anyone in it. The bear sat motionless, but the shadows behind him pulsed like breath.

"We have to go," Caleb said, voice low and urgent. "Now!"

Emma nodded, cradling Otis tight to her chest. He had stopped crying, but his tiny body trembled.

Behind them, something scraped across the floor—wood on wood, dragging.

Caleb turned toward it, raising the tire iron. "Get down the stairs. Now."

Emma didn't argue. *Thank fuck I grabbed my phone,* she thought as she fumbled one handed to cast light down the stairwell. She moved fast, nearly slipping on the narrow steps, Otis clutched tightly. Her heart hammered against his as they descended. Caleb backed down after her, eyes never leaving the attic room.

The door slammed shut behind him the moment his foot hit the landing.

They didn't wait to talk. Didn't check the nursery. Didn't gather things.

Emma grabbed her purse and the diaper bag sitting by the door to the garage. Caleb snatched the car keys from the kitchen counter. Daisy barked once, then bolted toward the garage like she already knew they were leaving.

They strapped Otis into his seat.

Emma was shaking and climbed into the back seat with the baby. No way did she want to be more than arm's reach away from him.

Caleb clamored into the driver's seat and started the car. He reached up and hit the garage door button. Nothing.

"Shit, damn power is out!"

Caleb jumped out to open the garage door manually, heaving the metal up, one loud inch at a time. It screeched in protest, heavy and stiff, jarring against the silence. Otis let out a startled cry. Emma whispered to him, bouncing slightly, desperate to calm him. The moment dragged. The door stuck once halfway. Caleb swore and yanked it harder until it finally opened.

Caleb was breathing in short, sharp gasps, as he backed out of the garage. He got to the road, narrowly missing the mailbox, and floored it.

The house loomed in the rearview mirror.

Neither of them looked back.

They didn't speak until they were halfway to the interstate. The baby had fallen asleep again, somehow. Daisy panted quietly between the seats.

"We'll figure out all the arrangements tomorrow." Caleb said finally.

Emma nodded, she was sobbing too hard to speak.

She stared out the window, one hand resting on Otis's chest, feeling every rise and fall.

And she wondered, without wanting to, how long they had before the bear found a way to follow.

They didn't stop until they reached a roadside motel—a beige, boxy place with buzzing neon and a half-lit vacancy sign. It smelled like bleach and old carpet, but the sheets were clean, they allowed dogs, and they were able to get a crib from the front desk.

Caleb carried the diaper bag and the car seat while Emma held Otis like a lifeline. Daisy followed behind.

Inside, they didn't speak much. Caleb double-locked the door and wedged a chair under the handle. Emma checked the motel crib three times before laying Otis inside. The baby stirred but stayed asleep, his fingers curled into tiny fists.

She sat on the edge of the bed, hands in her lap.

"We're safe," Caleb said, his voice frayed. "We're out. We did it."

Emma shook her head. "No. We got away. This time. That's not the same as safe."

Caleb looked like he wanted to argue but couldn't find the words.

She paced the motel room in bare feet. The carpet was flat and rough, the kind that didn't quite cushion but still held up despite years of use. The air was stale. She opened every drawer. Looked under the bed. Pulled back the shower curtain in the bathroom. Nothing. She stood in the middle of the room, twisting her wedding ring around her finger, trying to shake the feeling that something had followed them.

"It's a motel," Caleb said gently. "He can't find us here."

"How do you know!?" She opened the closet and looked up into the corners. Then she checked the space between the mattress and the wall. She didn't know what she expected to find. But she had to be sure.

"I keep thinking," Emma said softly, "we weren't supposed to see that room again. We weren't supposed to get him out."

"But we did," Caleb said. "You did."

The words rang hollow.

She didn't want credit. She wanted to forget—

but her brain wouldn't let her. The rocking chair. The way the crib had been moved up there. The way Cubby didn't flinch. Didn't need to.

"We'll call the real estate office tomorrow," Caleb said. "Hire movers. They can pack, too. We are *never* stepping foot in that place again."

Emma nodded. "We can't go back."

She rose and checked the door again. Then the windows. Otis still slept, unaware of the dark weight hanging over everything.

She stood there longer than she needed to, hand on the crib rail.

"Em, I think it's over," Caleb said gently.

"Will it ever be over?" she whispered.

She sat on the carpet beside Otis's crib with her knees pulled to her chest.

She wasn't watching the baby. She was watching the shadows.

And probably always would.

1995

THE BARN GROANED with the weight of its years. Wind pushed through the gaps in the siding, rattling loose boards like bones in a wooden ribcage. Dust danced in the high rafters, stirred by the approaching storm. The air inside was heavy with the scent of gasoline and old hay.

Richard stood at the center of it all, unmoving. The red gas can hung at his side, nearly empty. A lazy spiral of gasoline curled across the dirt and straw beneath his boots, dark and wet like ink freshly spilled. He inhaled. The sweetness of the fuel caught in his nose. Not unpleasant. Not anymore.

A boy whimpered behind him. He didn't bother to turn. His arms were pulled high above his head, wrists bound tight to the barn's central beam, the rope digging deep as his weight shifted. His gag was a folded kitchen towel, knotted tight. He'd stopped screaming an hour ago. His strength was waning. Now, his breath hitched in small, desperate bursts. He was eighteen, maybe twenty. Brown eyes. Dirt on his cheeks. Sneakers scuffed and damp. He didn't matter. Not in the way people *think* people matter. He was just the last one.

Richard knelt beside the hay bale where Cubby sat. The bear's fur was still perfect. Tan, soft, clean. The bow was a little off kilter, so Richard fixed it carefully, smoothing it out, centering it beneath the plush chin.

"It's just us now," he said, voice soft, almost childlike. "No one left to hurt us."

Cubby stared at him, almost disapprovingly, with his glass eyes.

"You said when she was gone, we could stop."

His mother had died six months ago. Almost to the day. He hadn't cried. Cirrhosis, the coroner said. She'd been found slumped in her recliner, a bottle of gin on the floor. Vomit down her front with the TV on, and an ashtray spilled into her lap. Her mouth had been open, eyes sunken, a cigarette still wedged between her fingers. The arm of the chair had scorched, but the flame had gone out on its own, like even the fire couldn't be bothered to finish her off. It had only burned long enough to sting the air and leave the arm of the chair scorched, the fabric shriveled and brittle to the touch.

Richard had found her. He didn't scream. He didn't feel anything while he stood in the doorway and stared at her corpse. He'd gone upstairs and told Cubby everything. And Cubby had promised there would be no more birthday parties.

"No more," Richard whispered. "That's what you said. No more after she was gone. That we could have some peace, and it would all be quiet."

He sat for a moment and let his eyes close.

And memories came.

The ferret was first. He was ten. His mother's boyfriend-of-the-month brought it home in a wire cage. Said it was "for fun." It stank. Scratched. Bit his fingers when he tried to pet it.

Richard had held it in his hands and pressed and

twisted until the little bones gave way. The body twitched and oozed. Cubby watched.

Two years later: Tommy. A neighbor boy. Nice enough kid. He had never been mean to Richard. But he was always following Richard around and yelling for him to come out and play. Cubby didn't like Richard to have friends. So, Richard had invited him over to play one last time, because Cubby had decided that he wanted to be rid of Tommy for *his* birthday.

Then Sean. *God, that kid was an asshole, but that was a memorable party.*

Marlene was later. She called Richard "Rick" and winked at him. She thought it was funny. It wasn't.

He had been careful. So careful. And patient. No one ever looked twice at him. How he hadn't been caught was a mystery to him. But the years had dulled the rush. What once felt like ritual now felt like obligation.

Richard opened his eyes. The barn creaked again, wind pressing against the walls like it wanted in. He stood, walked the spiral, checking the spread of gasoline. Flames would rise quickly. He knew the way wood burned. He'd read about airflow, flash-points. He was no amateur. He picked up the Polaroid camera, adjusted the strap around his neck.

"This is the last one," Richard said aloud, not to the boy, but to the bear. "I followed directions. I was good. I did everything right. So now we stop."

He approached the boy. He looked up, pleading through the tears, the snot, the damp cloth pressed to his mouth. Richard looked down at him, but he didn't *see* him. He saw time. Wasted years. Birthdays spent alone, with cold dinners and silence. The way his mother used to leave his gifts unwrapped, if she got him anything at all, tossed on the floor like afterthoughts. How the only constant—year after year—was Cubby.

The bear never left. Never scolded. Never hit him. Never told him he was too old, too strange, too quiet. He knelt, struck a match, and held it between them. The boy's eyes went wide. He tried to scream. Richard touched the flame to the trail of gasoline.

The fire came alive instantly—racing across the floor in a brilliant arc of orange and gold. Flames licked their way toward the outer beams. The barn moaned louder as the heat took hold. Richard didn't move.

He sat beside the boy and lifted the Polaroid. Cubby was placed gently between them, and he flipped the camera around.

"Smile," he whispered.

Click.

The flash went off. The moment captured.

Flames cracked behind them, painting their shadows huge across the walls. Smoke rolled upward, pooling at the ceiling.

The boy screamed behind the gag. Richard

closed his eyes. He felt the heat against his face. The sweat on his palms. The slow, even thud of his own heartbeat. He thought about the others.

Leah, with her soft voice and dreamy smile. Tina, who folded her laundry on Thursday nights. Carla, with her pink nails and bowling ball laugh.

All of them chosen. All of them remembered. Not for who they were, but how they fit into the shape of a story. And now, finally, the end. The barn roared. The heat became a living thing. Wood splintered above them. Smoke blackened the edges of the rafters. Embers rained down like sparks from some divine welder's torch. Still, Richard stayed. Didn't try to run. He was done.

"You said we could rest," he said, this time looking directly at Cubby. The bear did not reply. But he blinked.

The boy had stopped struggling. His breathing was ragged. Eyes fluttering. The heat pressed closer. Richard reached out, set the photo gently on the hay bale next to him. The image was still developing, but he knew what it would show.

Richard, the boy, and Cubby. Fire curling behind them. A final portrait. Another birthday finished. He sat back, placed one hand on Cubby's head, and gave a tired smile.

"Happy birthday, old friend," he said.

Outside, lightning flashed across the open sky.

And inside, the fire took everything.

THIRTEEN

The real estate agent led a couple through the main floor of the house, pointing out features and discussing the property's value. Their daughter, Lily—a curious eight-year-old with pigtails and a restless energy—grew bored with the adults' conversation about square footage and property taxes. *What is a kitchen renovation, anyway?* Earlier, the agent had said the "grown-up" bedroom was on the second floor, and as Lily's eyes glazed over from utter boredom, her parents exchanged a look. They knew that look.

"Just stay on the first floor, okay?" her dad had said. "We won't be long."

But Lily didn't care. Upstairs sounded better than whatever "interesting rates" were.

"They should call them boring rates," she mumbled.

She slipped away unnoticed while they lingered in the kitchen, listening to the agent drone on about granite counters and energy-efficient windows.

She wandered through the empty house, her footsteps echoing across the hardwood floors. Light streamed through the windows in long golden stripes, catching specks of dust in the air. Everything smelled like fresh paint and lemon cleaner, but beneath that lingered something older. Something dry and woody, like forgotten corners and quiet things.

She wandered through the dining room, ran her hand along the edge of a bare kitchen island, then spotted the stairs.

Upstairs sounded way better than countertops.

She tiptoed past the banister and started to climb, shoes whispering on the steps. Each creak made her giggle a little.

The second floor was quieter. Warmer. The carpet was pale and bare. She wandered down the hallway, peeking into the empty bedroom with sunlight slanting across the floor. Another room had a door that didn't open—it felt stuck. She knocked on it once, just to see if it would knock back. Nothing did.

In the hallway there were two closets, with a narrow door between them. It had been left slightly ajar. As she leaned to peek inside, she saw another set of stairs.

Lily looked over her shoulder. No one had followed her.

She grinned and opened it. All the way.

At the top of the shadowy staircase, was another door. It didn't look like part of a regular house. It looked like something out of a book—where secret passageways led to magical rooms or pirate treasure.

She ducked inside and climbed.

The stairs creaked softly beneath her light steps. With every one, the light faded a little more. The second floor gave way to dimness, and then to shadow. At the top, the attic waited—still and cool.

The attic was a space of deep shadows and dust motes dancing in narrow sunbeams from a single grimy window. The air was cooler here, heavier somehow, with a hush that made Lily instinctively quiet her breathing. Her fingers brushed over the rough wood of the door frame as she stepped inside.

The room had that old feeling—like time had folded in on itself. The kind of quiet that made you feel like you weren't alone, even when you were.

She took a few steps inside, nose wrinkling at the dry, sweet scent—like old wood and something faintly sweet. Maybe flowers? She couldn't tell. But it didn't smell like the rest of the house.

In the far corner, partially hidden in shadow, sat an old cedar chest. The wood was dark with age but smooth, its brass hinges still gleaming beneath a thin layer of dust. Something about it stood out.

"I knew it, I knew I'd find treasure!" She clapped her hands with delight.

Lily padded across the attic floor, pulled by the promise of something magical. She knelt and ran her hands over the warm grain of the lid. It was warmer than the surrounding room.

She hesitated, then opened it.

The hinges creaked softly.

Inside, nestled alone on the cedar bottom, sat a teddy bear. It was light brown, with shiny black glass eyes and a perfectly tied blue velvet bow. The bear looked soft and brand new, impossibly clean for something found in a dusty old attic.

She studied it for a moment, then smiled. It felt like he belonged to her, like he'd been waiting for her to find him.

She reached in and picked him up. The bear was heavier than she expected. Warm—not sun-warm, but skin-warm. She didn't think about why. The bear looked like he wanted to be hugged close.

His fur was soft against her cheek.

"Mom! Dad! Look what I found!" she called, forgetting she'd probably be in trouble for coming up here. Her voice echoing upward toward the rafters, then downward through the house.

Footsteps clattered on the stairs below. Lily turned toward the attic door, bear tucked tightly under her chin, one hand still stroking the velvety bow at his neck.

Her parents appeared a moment later, both a little breathless. Her mom put a hand on her chest and let out a laugh. "Lily! You scared me half to death."

The agent poked her head up behind them, smiling politely but clearly flustered. "We ask people not to explore up here without an agent. Some of the flooring's uneven."

Lily's dad chuckled and ruffled her hair. "Leave it to this one to find the one place in the entire house she's not supposed to go."

"But look!" Lily, beaming with joy, held up the teddy bear. "His name is Cubby! I think he was waiting for me."

Her mom exchanged a smile with the agent. "She's got an eye for buried treasures."

"Can we live here? Can I keep him? The lady said you'll get a good interesting rate!"

Her parents exchanged a glance and laughed. Lily pulled the bear into a hug, holding it tight to her chest.

"You're mine, "she whispered.

And with his fluffy face now looking over her shoulder, where no one could see—he blinked once.

Slow.

Deliberate.

And Cubby waited.

ACKNOWLEDGMENTS

Writing this book was like inviting a haunted bear to live in my brain rent-free. It whispered things at all hours. It made a mess, knocked things over, and refused to leave quietly until I wrote this story. It lingered in the corners, breathing down my neck while I worked. It didn't care about outlines or deadlines. It wanted blood. And it wasn't going anywhere until it got it.

Now for the hard part: trying to list everyone I'd like to thank. Honestly, it's impossible. So many people showed up for me in quiet, essential ways—through group chats, coffee, memes, chaos, and friendship. If you're wondering whether you're on this list, you probably are. And I'm so, so grateful. 🐻

To my editor, Darren "Ninetoes" Perdue: He claims he's "just the average reader." This is a *lie*. Darren has an eye for detail, a sharp sense of story, and is an absolute grammar gremlin. This book is cleaner and more consistent because of him. 🦌

To my besties, Savannah and Julia (and *sometimes* Barbara): you are my lifeline, my sounding board, and my favorite kind of chaos. Thank you for reading my drafts at odd hours, cheering me on, talking me down, and always being on board with every unhinged idea. Absolute legends.

To Lisa, Kat, and John: thank you for diving headfirst into my insanity. You saw Cubby before he was fully stitched together and still encouraged me to keep going. Your insights, support, and "what's wrong with you" messages mean the world. (F4L!)

To caffeine, intrusive thoughts, and the sheer spite that drives my writing—thank you for fueling chaos, creativity, and exactly zero healthy sleep habits.

To the readers—thank you for picking up this book and following me into the attic. I probably owe you a bundle a of sage and a nightlight. If your teddy bear give you the creeps now . . . my work here is done.

And finally, to Cubby. Please stay in the book. Please.

—Jyl Glenn
06 July 2025

About the Author

Jyl Glenn is a horror writer, editor, formatter, narrator, and mentor. She collects creepy art, writes really depressing poetry, loves dogs, and has an affinity for pink dinosaurs. She is forever a New Yorker who happens to live in Tulsa now.

Newsletter, signed books, and unhinged merch:
www.jylglennwrites.com

f facebook.com/jylglenn

○ instagram.com/_delightfully_unhinged_

ALSO BY JYL GLENN

<u>Book and Anthologies</u>

Burns of Horror

Netipotcalypse: A Collaborative Novel

Crumpled: Stories From the Horror Archives

Phobophobia: Face Your Fears

<u>Coming Soon</u>

The Writing on The Wall: A Horror Tribute to Iron Maiden
(October 3, 2025)

<u>Other Publications</u>

"Ozark Mist," in *Hootenanny Horrorshow*, ed. RJ Roles
(From the Ashes, 2024), 165

"The Algorithm," in *Error Code*, ed. Zaq Cass (Rabid Otter
Horror, 2024), 83

"The Secret Ingredient," in *Tales from the Lark Side*, ed.
Lindsey Goddard (Weird Wide Web, 2025)

<u>Poetry</u>

"The Cage," in *Sleeve of Hearts*, ed. Lindsey Goddard
(Weird Wide Web, 2024), 52